A tale of flaming love,
treachery, and sudden, savage warfare in the pueblos
of the ancient southwest
—told by a master writer
of adventure
stories.

# DAUGHTER
## of the Sun

## Johnston McCulley

FICTION HOUSE PRESS

**Fiction House Edition December 2020**

"Daughter of the Sun" was first published as a three-part serial in *The Argosy* pulp magazine in issues dated May 4, May 11, and May 18, 1918. Copyright by the Frank A. Munsey Company in 1918. The story was reprinted in the *Akron Beacon Journal* and the *Bangor Daily News* newspapers in 1940. This book contains the newspaper text.

isbn 978-1-64720-202-6

Fiction House Press
www.FictionHousePress.com

# DAUGHTER OF THE SUN

## CHAPTER I

NOW the sun touched the peaks to the east with glory, and the sky brightened and the day came, and far below the billows of mist rose and scattered and the cool night-breath of the desert was gone.

The dark purple in the foothills faded. In the pueblo dogs began to bark as their masters came from the community houses to stretch their arms, breathe deep the bracing air, and face the new day. Children shrieked and chattered. The air suddenly was heavy with the odors of cooking food.

But these things near at hand did not call for the attention of the watcher. He stood high on the look-out rock, outlined against the brightening sky, where all the pueblo could see him. To the east and north he could see the great range of rough mountains that men in days to come would call the Rockies. To the south and west stretched the sun-baked mesa, touched here and there with tiny stretches of green, where small streams flowed—a puzzling land that men in ages yet unborn would call New Mexico.

Like a bronze statue he stood, tall and straight, his arms rigid at his sides, his chin lifted, his body balanced nicely on the balls of his feet.

Each morning the watcher stood so and looked upon this picture, for his was a post of great honor. His eyes were such that he could see twice as far as any ordinary man. The cacique himself had appointed him to the post, and the sun-priest had blessed him.

And so throughout the long day he watched, having food brought to him by one of the temple maidens when the sun was directly overhead, and the great gong called upon those of the pueblo to pause a moment in their work and worship.

He watched the desert trails that none might approach unheralded to challenge the peace of the pueblo. He watched for spent runners who might lie down exhausted to die—their messages undelivered. He watched the heavens that he might give warning of the coming of storms. In all the great pueblo there was no man quite so important as Bruxoli, the watcher, though the cacique and the sun-priest might have said differently.

Now he turned his face toward the west, looking down the main trail in the direction of the Red Pueblo, a thing he hated and could not see, and for a moment his inscrutable expression vanished arid a look of rage was in its place. Over the trail the mist-billows were rolling, and soon the black heat-waves would be there instead, and through them would come the haughty Lazzano, son of the cacique of the Red Pueblo, a man admired by many and despised by some.

He would come in a manner befitting a cacique's son, striding at the head of half a score of men, great bracelets of gold upon his arms and many brilliant feathers in his headdress. Runners had arrived the evening before with news of his approach. And down in the pueblo there had been merry-making and feasting, for all knew the reason for his coming.

The watcher knew it, too, and he thought of it now as his eyes searched the west for the thing he did not wish to see. He knew that down in the temple the sun-priest was ready, and that at dawn the next day Lazzano would wed Dezla, the daughter of the sun, for so the cacique had ordered, being a man who did not hesitate to sacrifice his daughter if more power politically was to be gained through doing it.

Something like a sob came from the watcher's breast as the mist rolled away from the trail and its length lay before his eyes. The love he held for the daughter of the sun must be stifled, of course, for he was not of noble birth, yet he would have seen her wed to a more worthy man. Lazzano, the prince, had a reputation throughout the desert that guaranteed he would make no woman happy.

There was no speck of black on the wide trail now to indicate the bridegroom's approach and Bruxoli, the watcher, gave a sigh of relief and turned to look toward the east. Below him he heard the excited chatter of those in the pueblo, and he condescended to glance down.

On the ledge below men and women and children had gathered, and they were looking toward the watcher. He thought at first that it was because they wanted him to signal whether or not the prince was in sight.

And then he saw that the top of the long ladder was trembling—the ladder that ran to the crest of the lookout rock, and up which no person was permitted to climb without special permission from the cacique lest the watcher be beguiled from his duty.

Perhaps it was the sun-priest, he thought, come with special orders, for the cacique was too old and infirm to climb such a distance himself. Or perhaps, because this was to be the wedding day of the daughter of the sun, some special food was being sent up to him before the hour of the midday sun.

Because of the dignity of his position he turned away from the top of the ladder and stood straight again, facing toward the west, and a man would have said that he scarcely breathed. He had the right to remain thus until spoken to, and even then it was his privilege to glance at the trail again and take his time about replying.

He heard quick, sharp breathing behind him—heard a step on the rock, and knew that his visitor had reached the summit. But Bruxoli did not turn his eyes from the west trail. He was looking toward the distant hills, watching for the black speck on the mesa that would tell of the approach of Lazzano.

"Bruxoli," said a soft voice behind him then.

He thrilled at the word and forgot the dignity of his position and the fact that he could show his authority by refusing to turn for a moment, or so. He whirled around with a glad cry on his lips and a smile on his face.

"Dezla, daughter of the sun!" he cried, and knelt on one knee before her and bent his head.

"The watcher need not kneel to me," she said. "Stand erect and look me in the face, Bruxoli."

DEZLA, the daughter of the sun, was as brilliant as the dazzling god they worshipped. Slight of form she was and deep bronze in color, and her black hair fell far below her waist, and her black eyes snapped continually, either with pleasure or with anger.

She laughed and sprang forward, up beside the watcher, and looked out over the desert, stretching her arms out to the great world.

And then the heart of Bruxoli saddened suddenly, and the bright look left his face, for he thought he knew the reason for her coming.

"Is the daughter of the sun then so eager for a husband?" he asked.

"Bruxoli!" she cried, turning to face him. "Until you spoke 1 had forgotten the day and what it might mean to me. 1 came here because I love the world, and the other day I heard the sun-priest saying how fair it looked from the watcher's rock. Times without number, after I had started to climb. I was of a mind to turn back, for the task was no easy one, and the people gathered below and called to me. But 1 wanted to see the world, and I knew that the watcher was here—and would protect me."

"I humbly crave your pardon, Dezla!" Bruxoli said. "But this thing is sore against my heart—"

"Then you do not wish to see your princess a wife and happy?"

"Most of all do I wish to see her happy, but I fear that Lazzano cannot make her so."

"Those are bold words for one not of noble birth."

"Yet they are true words, my princess. I have heard tales of this Lazzano—who has not?"

"You believe these things?" she asked.

"Knowing them for the truth, my princess. Once, when I was a runner—before the cacique, your father, gave me my position here—I came across him in one of his orgies, far from the Red Pueblo, where he has his home. He is no fit husband for the daughter of the sun!"

"And so you would not have me wed with him because he is given to such things! Is that the only reason, Bruxoli?"

"My princess—" he stammered.

"Answer me!" she cried, "It is the only reason?"

"A man of my birth may not speak of love to the daughter of the sun. Yet I would not have you think 1 hate this Lazzano because of a jealousy. Were he worthy, I would watch you wed him with good grace, though my heart burned for you!"

He spoke and turned away and looked far down the desert trail.

"At least your love is true and worthy, Bruxoli," she said. "But a woman may not guide her heart nor select her father. Were 1 not the daughter of the sun—and loved you—"

"My princess!"

"Even were you noble I could not love you, Bruxoli. I respect you, admire you, feel safe in your presence, but love—it is something more than that. Your face does not haunt my dreams. I do not long for the feel of your hand, the song of your voice. And these things would come to pass did I love you."

"These things come to pass when you think of Lazzano?" he asked, rather bewildered.

"Not so, Bruxoli! I have no love for the prince from the Red Pueblo. I, too, have heard the stories. But what can a girl do when her father is a great cacique and gives his commands? This is my last bit of freedom and happiness-—up here on the top of the world with you, my watcher. At dawn tomorrow, they say, I shall stand before the sun-priest with Lazzano, who has admired my beauty and has had his father intrigue to buy me from mine!"

"My princess!"

"And, being the daughter of the sun, I must go to my bridal with some semblance of happiness, for all in the pueblo will be watching. 'Tis a part of being a princess to smile when the heart is breaking. If it were so that something could happen—"

"What is it you will to happen, my princess?"

"Two things, oh, watcher! That this Lazzano does not come to claim me for bride. And that there will come a day when the sight of a man will make my heart sing a perpetual song—and that I shall wed him. Two things—that can never be!"

"The sun-god is powerful!"

"I have entreated him, but there has been no answer. Perhaps in the past 1 have angered him—and this is my punishment. I think that must be it, O watcher, for yesterday at midday 1 tried to look him in the face and make my silent supplication—and could not. He blazed with such anger that 1 was forced to turn my eyes away. And for a long time afterward I could see his image in my eyes, though I did not look at him again directly."

"What could my princess do to anger the god'?" Bruxoli asked.

"Perhaps it Is because I have wished for so much happiness," she replied. "It may be wrong to be happy. The sun-priest is a holy man, and I am sure he is not happy, for he never smiles, and his lips do not know how to sound a laugh—to fashion a smile, even. And if the priest cannot be happy, how can a simple maiden?"

The watcher was looking out over the desert again. He was thinking of many things, and presently one of them bubbled off his lips.

"If this Lazzano were not to arrive from the Red Pueblo—" he said.

"Last night came runners saying that he was on his way and would arrive before the sun sets again."

"If he were met between here and there by a man who would give up his life to make a woman happy—"

"What mean you, Bruxoli?" she asked, frightened.

"Perchance, if the watcher should meet him, spear in hand, or fire an arrow from ambush—"

"Bruxoli—the deed could not be done! You are the watcher, and for you to leave your post means death. They would see you from the pueblo and give chase—and the sun-priest would be passing judgment on you before ever you had drawn breath from your first running."

"The watcher knows the desert, my princess. He knows a way to the floor of it that does not go down through the pueblo. Bruxoli can pass down the opposite side of the lookout rock, clutching to jagged ends with his hands and bare feet, and so reach the trail."

"They would notice that you were not on the summit. They know that I am up here looking at the world. They would sound the alarm."

"I could reach the trail and speed along it. In some likely place I could meet this prince of the Red Pueblo—this beast who would force a woman to wed him. With a single shot I can save you, my princess! My arrow will speed true!"

"And then—" she asked.

"Then there will be those of his escort to be reckoned with. It will be impossible to flee, for he has some great runners with him. Nor will Bruxoli be taken alive—to be carried to the Red Pueblo and tortured by the cacique he has robbed of an unworthy son! My knife of flint is very sharp—and my heart beats just beneath my ribs!"

"You would do this for me?" she breathed.

"And regret that I could not do more, my princess."

"And do you think I would have the death of such a man upon my hands?" she asked. "It is better that I have a husband I despise than that you should lose your honorable post and your life."

"I do not choose to think so. There may be happiness in death; there would be none at all for you if you wed this Lazzano. My princess, let me go!"

"I cannot! Your blood would be upon my hands!"

"I must save you!"

"Perhaps it would not save me, Bruxoli. The people of the pueblo know I am here with you. They would say that I had sent you to slay this prince. My father would be angry—and the cacique of the Red Pueblo would be enraged. He might even demand my life in payment, and, I think, my father would grant it—for my father is old, and did he not remain the friend of the Red Pueblo's chief he would be deposed."

"The tyrant of the Red Pueblo will not always rule the world!" Bruxoli cried. "Some day a man will come to lead us against him!"

"I think my father hates me a little because I am a girl," she said. "Had I been his son instead of his daughter there would be a man now, in my father's old age, to lead our people!"

"Is there not some other way?" the watcher asked. "Can I not strike him down as he enters the temple?"

"Bruxoli! And have the sun-god consume you with fire for the sacrilege?"

"If it would insure your happiness-'

"Could I be happy, knowing that a brave man had gone to death for me?"

"Daughter of the sun—command me to do it!" he begged.

"It is too late," she said. "I must obey my father's will! And see—the bridegroom comes!"

She pointed toward the west. The watcher saw a black speck against the glare of the desert

"My princess!" he begged again.

"It is too late," she said. "The bridegroom comes. It is fate, oh, watcher! For see—the sun-god smiles! The god is pleased, oh, watcher, that 1 am to wed this unworthy man! It must be a punishment for some sin!"

## CHAPTER II

**B**RUXOLI knelt before her and touched her hand, and then she left him and ran rapidly to the top of the ladder. There she stopped to smile at him again, and then she began going down the rungs.

The watcher choked back a sob and took his place upon the lookout rock, and again he gazed out over the desert and up the trail at the tiny black speck in the distance.

Assured that the black object moved in the direction of the pueblo, the watcher held both hands high above his head, thus giving the signal. Below in the pueblo a great gong struck, and the guards ran to their places as was their custom when the watcher gave notice of somebody's approach.

Having signalled the arrival, Bruxoli turned and looked toward the trails that ran east, disdaining to witness the approach of the prince of the Red Pueblo, to the neglect of his other duties. It seemed, too, that he could not look at Lazzano in all his haughty splendor—for in his breast he knew that he hated the man who was to wed the daughter of the sun.

Dezla went on down the long ladder, smiling roguishly at the advice those below bellowed up at her. Now and then she pretended to miss a step, and the people of the pueblo gasped in horror, and the old cacique, her father, almost passed away because of his fear for her.

But finally she reached the topmost shelf and turned to look down at them from this point of comparative safety, waving her hands and laughing once more.

Then she ran rapidly down the shorter ladder and stood in their midst.

"Dezla—daughter of the sun!" her father cried in his weak voice. "You have played with death!"

"The climb was nothing." she replied. "And I have looked out over the world."

"The watcher has given the signal."

"Yes. One comes," she said.

"One? There is no escort?"

"I did not mean the words that way, my father. It was impossible for even the watcher, with his keen eyes, to see. 'Tis but a black speck far up the trail, but it moves toward the pueblo."

"And my daughter is happy that the bridegroom comes—so happy that she climbs the lookout rock to catch first glimpse of him?"

Her father's voice trembled as he spoke, for he loved this daughter of his, and regretted that political circumstances were such that he was forced to give her to Lazzano, and down in his heart he hoped that Dezla was a willing bride, for it would be better so.

"Did I show too much eagerness?" the girl asked by way of reply. She did not wish to hurt her old father and his deep pride by showing that Lazzano would not be welcome.

"He must be received with all honor, the cacique said now, looking at the nobles about him. "This sun-priest has decorated the temple, and do you men of good names be ready to greet this prince when he comes in off the trail."

They bowed before their cacique and backed away to do his bidding, though they had small stomach for it.

Well these nobles knew the reputation of Lazzano, prince of the Red Pueblo; and while they were not outspoken, as was Bruxoli, the watcher, yet they had certain feelings in the matter. And more than one of them had sought to wed Dezla himself.

The sun-priest came to the door of the temple, and the cacique went slowly across to him and stood beside him on the steps, while slaves placed his chair.

"All is ready, cacique," the sun-priest said. "This prince of the Red Pueblo will make his prayers, and then there shall be feasting throughout the long night. And at the first streak of dawn in the new day the ceremony shall take place."

"It is a bitter thing!" the old cacique said.

"It is," the sun-priest replied. "Evil days have fallen upon our people when we must bow to the cacique of the Red Pueblo and give our daughter of the sun to his profligate offspring. Were there a man to lead us—"

"There is none such!" the cacique said. "And without generalship we would but die like curs—else bend our necks to the feet of the Red Pueblo's cacique. Let us hope that the daughter of the sun will look upon her husband with favor, and that the sun-god will grant that he love her so much that he will mend his profligate ways!"

The priest turned away to give orders to the maidens of the temple, who had the decorations in charge. He, too, hated the prince of the Red Pueblo, who once had flouted him in public. And he hated the prince's father because of his political prestige, for were his own cacique the more powerful, then he would be the more powerful priest.

Now those on the shelf saw the watcher giving more signs, and they called out, and the priest hurried to the door of the temple again. Bruxoli had his arms extended at his sides, and was whirling rapidly on the toes of one foot. The priest struck the gong to show that the signal had been seen.

"Trouble!" he mused.

"What was it?" the cacique asked.

"The watcher is signalling that there is trouble."

"Out to the trail!" the cacique commanded those of his guard who attended him. "Meet the prince of the Red Pueblo and give him aid! It will be an ill day for us if he meets with bad fortune!"

The guards hurried away, running swiftly along the ledge to the big ladders, their spears and shields and arrowcases rattling. At a respectable distance from the door of the temple the people of the pueblo crowded together, wondering what was to come. The daughter of the sun passed through them and approached her father.

"There is trouble?" she asked.

"I know not its nature. The watcher gave the signal. Perhaps a man of the prince's escort has fallen by the wayside. In his eagerness to arrive and claim you, Lazzano may have worked his carriers too hard."

"That were cruel," she said. "And it is not necessary, my father. The ceremony is not to be until tomorrow's dawn."

"Lazzano loves to feast, and he knows well we have prepared entertainment for him."

"Yes, Lazzano loves to feast." she agreed, and

there was something in her voice that caused the old cacique to look up at her swiftly. He wanted to feel sure that the daughter of the sun would be happy in her bridal, and her voice sounded as if there was grave doubt of it.

From the end of the shelf there came a babble of sound now, and the guards began pushing the people back. The sun-priest stood aside so that he could look down to the ladders. More guards swarmed up, and one of them carried upon his back a man. But when the shelf was reached this man forced them to put him down on the rock, and thus held between two of them he approached the door of the temple.

They could see that he was tall and strong, and his breast labored with his breath as if he had run far and at great speed. He prostrated himself before the cacique, fighting to get breath enough to speak, and the captain of the guard made his report.

"He fell exhausted as we reached him," he said. "He gasped out something about a story for the cacique's ears. There is a wound across his shoulders, and it looks as if an arrow had streaked him there."

"WHAT is your story?" the cacique demanded, touching the prostrate man with his foot.

The man raised his head as the sun-priest stepped closer. The daughter of the sun was standing close beside her father's chair for she seemed to sense that this thing had to do with her.

She beheld the runner's face as he looked at the cacique. A strong face it was, and a handsome one, made to go well with the man's wonderful body.

The runner was speaking.

"O great cacique. It is ill news I carry!" he said.

"Say on!"

"Two dawns ago, after a night of feasting, Prince Lazzano left the Red Pueblo on his journey here to claim the daughter of the sun as his bride. He had with him an escort of 10 men, including his guard and runners. Two runners he dispatched to you at different times, which left but eight in his party besides himself. Last night there was a camp so that the prince might be refreshed for the last part of his journey. An hour before dawn he moved forward again, and when the sun came he worshipped with his men. We came to a curve in the trail, where it winds around a great rock the sun-god built in the desert ages ago. As the prince reached the great rock, an arrow sped from a heap of boulders near by. The prince staggered and fell, O cacique, for the arrow had passed through his heart. The man among the boulders shot truly."

"Dead? Prince Lazzano dead?" the cacique cried, so that all of the pueblo heard.

"Instantly dead, O, cacique! The eight men of his escort rushed forward, even the runners who have not been trained as soldiers and are not supposed to make war. A second arrow came from the boulders, and a second man fell.

"Then the battle began. A. cloud of arrows were sent toward the boulders, and with spears in their hands the men charged. But the hidden marksman cut them down, O, cacique one at a time, the last when he had almost reached the rocks."

"All dead?" the cacique cried.

"All," the runner answered. "All in that fight are dead, with the exception of myself."

"And you—"

"I had an arrow across the back—you can see the wound. And in the excitement I was struck against the side of the head with the butt of a spear. I dropped as if dead, O cacique. and for a time knew nothing. When my senses returned to me I found dead men on every side. I made my way to the boulders, but the man who had been in them was gone. Only a few broken arrows remained. And on the breast of the prince was a message."

"A message?" the cacique cried.

"It was painted on a bit of skin, cacique. I have it here, that you may see. It reads: 'By the grace of Tanlu, the outcast!' "

"Tanlu!" cried the cacique and the sun priest in a breath.

"Tanlu!" murmured the daughter of the sun, as if praising the name.

"Yes, cacique! It was Tanlu, the outcast, who slew the prince and his men. Why he did it, 1 know not, yet I think he must have been angered at the prince for something. And Prince Lazzano is dead—and Tanlu lives. And I stand in fear of vengeance!"

But the cacique was not thinking now of the man who had brought the story. He was thinking of Tanlu, and the sun priest was thinking of Tanlu, and so were the people who had heard the message.

The name of Tanlu was something mothers used with which to frighten naughty children. Tanlu, the outcast, struck terror to the hearts of those in the pueblos. While yet a boy he had been cast forth because in his anger he had slain a playmate. The broad desert was his home, and a poor hut his house, men supposed. But Tanlu, coming to the strength of manhood, did not keep a few goats and raise a few roots upon which to live. He became a menace of the trails.

Runners had been found dead in the desert, and it was blamed on Tanlu. It was well known that he approached a pueblo now and then, and took what pleased him. And when men pursued they died. For Tanlu, knowing the far stretches of country, shot and killed, and sped away, and no man could follow.

Once the cacique of the Red Pueblo had sent after him a body of soldiers, but while they searched the desert Tanlu invaded the Red Pueblo alone and took a box of precious stones from the cacique's treasure house, leaving his sign behind him.

None knew what features this Tanlu had, for he

wrapped his long hair about his face when he went on a raid. Legend had it that he was a tall man, with the strength of a mountain lion in his long frame. Men about to make a journey prayed the sun god to keep Tanlu from their trail.

The people began wailing, and Dezla bent her head, and they thought she was struggling to keep back the tears, when in reality she was hiding her smiles and her happiness.

For the sun god had favored her. Two wishes she had made—that she would not be the bride of Lazzano, and that some day a man would stir her heart and she would wed him. And the first had come to pass.

"Sanctuary, O priest!" the man who had brought the message was crying now. "The cacique of the Red Pueblo will have me slain if I take him news of his son's death! And I had no blame in it!"

The sun priest pulled at his long hair and regarded the man.

He knew that the messenger spoke the truth. The cacique of the Red Pueblo was a brutal man, and he counted the life of a slave as nothing.

"You shall have sanctuary!" the priest declared. Not only did he wish to save the life of an innocent man, but also he would show his authority to the cacique of the Red Pueblo. Even a cacique could not offer harm to a man who bore the sanctuary mark on his forehead. Such a thing would be an affront to the god himself!

"You shall have sanctuary!" he cried again; and from a pouch at his belt he took a metal box, and opened it, and dipped his finger into a liquid there. He motioned for the man to approach and kneel and hold up his head, and with his finger he made two parallel lines on the man's forehead—two lines in red that would stain the skin forever.

"You now have sanctuary!" the priest said. "No man may offer you harm without he affront the god. You may come and go with honor among the people of any pueblo, and none dare raise hand against you. For the mark of the god is on your brow, and every temple is your home!"

The man sprang to his feet. His happy laugh rang out and struck all within hearing with astonishment.

"It is done! It is done!" he cried. "Not even the sun priest may efface the mark!"

## CHAPTER III

THE messenger entered the temple to refresh himself and to rest, and the cacique called his guard about him, and summoned his swiftest runner. The sun priest prepared a statement of the tragedy, and fastened it to the runner's belt, and bade him go with all speed to the Red Pueblo and to the cacique there, and give him news of Lazzano's untimely death.

But before the man went away the priest painted the parallel lines on his forehead, for it was like the cacique to slay the messenger when he had given the news, and such a slaying might be the excuse for war.

Dezla had retired to the apartment of the daughter of the sun in the temple, and the people thought she mourned for her bridegroom, whereas she hid herself in order that they might not see the happiness shining in her eyes and think it unseemly.

She was eager to send word to the watcher of what had come to pass, but of course she could not climb the lookout rock again herself under the circumstances, and she knew it might cause talk if she asked her father to send one of the guard.

The maidens of the temple, sympathizing as they supposed. with her stricken love, bathed her brows with scented water and gave her food arid drink, and then she sent them away.

The hours passed slowly. She heard the people chanting when the great gong on the roof of the temple was struck at the midday hour, and knew that they were praying that she might yet be happy, and she felt a little ashamed because she had not let them understand.

Once the sun priest visited her, but she told him that all was well and that she had no need of his ministrations. Perhaps the priest guessed that all was not sorrow in the heart of the daughter of the sun, for his eyes were twinkling when he blessed her. But the twinkle died away and his brow furrowed when he considered what the cacique of the Red Pueblo might do.

The long afternoon passed and the evening shadows came, and Dezla remained in the temple, as was her privilege, for she was not ready to face the people yet. Then came the darkness, and an early full moon covered the desert with glory, and she knew that Bruxoli, the watcher had ceased his vigil, and that another man stood in his place until one hour before the dawn.

Dezla left the seclusion of the chamber set apart for the daughter of the sun and went out into the great main room of the temple. She glanced up at the round hole in the roof, through which the sun god sent his beams each midday, and saw that the moon was smiling through it now. And because of its light the interior of the edifice looked ghostly.

There were great pillars that held up the heavy roof, and there was a flight of steps cut from the living stone that led to the altar of the sun.

It came into the mind of Dezla that she had not given thanks enough, and she walked slowly to the bottom of the flight of steps, and knelt there, and looked up at the spot where the sun god smiled when it was day.

"O master of all light!" she breathed. "Dezla thanks you from her heart! Thy daughter humbles herself before thee, because thou hast done this thing. And grant me, master of all light, what else I crave, if it is not a sin to have happiness!"

Her heart beat faster as she spoke, for she realized that she was asking the god to send her a man who would make her heart sing and grant her that she wed him. Thrice she bowed her head until it touched the stone of the bottom step, and then she got up quickly and turned to go away.

A shadow stepped from one of the great pillars, and a man spoke: "Dezla! Daughter of the sun!"

And she raised her head quickly and looked at him, and saw that he was the messenger who had brought the news of Prince Lazzano's death, and who had been given sanctuary..

"You have been praying to the god?" she asked.

The man stepped nearer, and now the moonlight revealed his features' clearly, and she could see that he was smiling.

"I never forget to pray to the god at the proper time," he made answer. "But I have not been praying to him just now."

"You are passing through the temple?" she asked.

This man was very good to look upon, she was telling herself. It seemed to her that her breath came quicker when she looked into his eyes and saw the sparkle there.

Since he was a runner, he must be a slave, yet he did not act as one.

"I have been watching you at your prayers," he said.

"That were a bold thing for a slave to do!"

"I am no slave, daughter of the sun—at least not a slave to man. Am I slave at all, it is to thy grace and beauty."

" 'Tis a pretty speech, but you are bold to make it," she said, with something of displeasure in her voice.

"Boldness is a quality all men should have."

"It would become you better did you show some sorrow because of the death of your master," she rebuked him.

"Does Dezla, the daughter of the sun, grieve because her bridegroom will not come?"

"This passes the limit of safety!" she said. "Shall I call a guard and have you chastised for your words?"

"Yet my question remains unanswered. I am a man who sees beyond the end of my nose, sweet Dezla. Let the men and women of the pueblo believe that you are weeping in sorrow, for appearance must be upheld, but allow me, gracious one, to have knowledge of the truth."

"What mean you?"

"Did not your heart beat with happiness when you heard my message regarding Prince Lazzano? Were you not glad that the roisterer would not claim you as bride? Did you not feel a moment's thanks to that Tanlu, the outcast, for what he had done?"

"Feel thanks for a man like Tanlu?" she gasped.

"And why not?"

"Why not? Thou hast not heard the true story, daughter of the sun. Tanlu was but a boy in years when he lived at the big pueblo of the south that the shaking of the earth wrecked years ago. He cut the heart of the man who annoyed his sister, and he was deemed outcast, for the man he killed was a cousin of the cacique.

"So he went into the open desert to live with the rats and lizards."

"It were a sorrowful tale," she said, "if it were true."

"It is true, daughter of the sun! And there he grew to be a man, making friends of other outcasts, and learning the secrets of the open country, and in time he became like a king. King of the Outcasts. he called himself!"

"But his crimes—"

"Never has he murdered a man except by way of honest revenge. In all his life never has he wronged a woman. All crimes committed by men others believe honest have been blamed on Tanlu. He has stolen at times that he might live. He has taken wealth and goods from other men who have robbed the poor. And on the other side, he has done much good. The lives of outcasts he has saved. He has appeared from nowhere into the midst of the desert and given cool water to dying men who had done him no wrong. He has slipped into the pueblos at night, ofttimes, and given to the poor what he has taken from the rich."

"NEVER before have I heard of such things."

"That is because men are slow to speak well of one of whom once they spoke evil," he explained. "And now this Tanlu, the outcast, hath done thee a service, perhaps."

"Here in the temple, I do not deny thee the right to know," she said. "It was not in my heart to wed Lazzano of the Red Pueblo."

Then Tanlu has done well?"

"Perhaps he has done well," she said. "But I forget. You were of Prince Lazzano's escort; you may carry word of this to the cacique who was his father."

"Trust me, Dezla of the sun. I hated Prince Lazzano with an abiding hatred. He was not a proper man for you."

"Did Tanlu hate him too, that he shot him down from ambush?"

"There is a story about it," he said. They were sitting now, at the bottom of the steps, and he bent forward and she could feel his breath upon her throat.

"I—I will hear the story."

"Once Tanlu slipped into this pueblo, to take food to a poor family who had been robbed and were too proud to ask of the common pot. It was a feast evening, and so he was unobserved. He left the food, and then he mingled in the throng. And then he saw Dezla of the sun."

"He saw me?"

"And declared that the sun god himself was not half so radiant! He watched her as much as he dared, and that night, after the feasting was at an end, he crept away into the desert again, around the guards, with her image in his heart."

"Tanlu did that?" she gasped, happily.

"Yes, daughter of the sun, Tanlu did that. And often, then, he came to the pueblo, risking danger of capture and execution, for as you know there is a law that if an outcast enter a pueblo he must die. And often he saw Dezla of the sun, and his heart almost burst for love of her. But she was the only child of the cacique, and chief of the temple maidens also, and, of course, he dared not speak of his love."

"Of course not," she agreed.

"And then he heard that Dezla was to wed Lazzano of the Red Pueblo, and he knew that Lazzano was unworthy, and he believed that Dezla did not crave the match. He knew that the cacique, her father, was old and weak, and that the cacique of the Red Pueblo made threats of invasion if the marriage did not take place. And he disliked to see Dezla of the sun sacrificed to an unworthy man."

"How did he know all these things?" Dezla asked.

"Tanlu knows many things, and has many ways of finding them out. So he went down to the trail and waited there for the prince and his escort to arrive on their journey to the wedding, and single-handed, he slew this Lazzano and his escort, that Dezla, the beautiful daughter of the sun, might be free!"

"And I thank this Tanlu!" she whispered. "Perhaps it is a sin to say it, but I am not grieving that Lazzano is dead."

"Why should you? He was not worthy your thought!"

"You speak strangely of your dead master," she said.

"He was no master of mine!"

"You were of his escort."

"No!"

"But you were! You brought us the news of the tragedy! You had a wound yourself! Who are you? How do you know what has passed in the mind of Tanlu, the outcast?"

"I brought the news—yes! The cut across my back I made with my own spear! I brought the news—because it would give me a chance to see Dezla of the sun and watch the happiness creep back into her face when she learned that she would not have to wed Lazzano! As for the mind of Tanlu—I know it all!"

"You are one of his men? You, too, are an outcast?"

"No outcast, but a man who has been given sanctuary. And I am no man of Tanlu's. He has no men. He leads no band of outlaws, as some men say. Tanlu has righted his wrongs alone; always he stands alone! Do you not understand?"

"Understand what?" she asked.

He bent nearer, he knelt on one knee before her.

"I, myself, am Tanlu!" he said.

"You?"

The daughter of the sun recoiled a space and gazed at him in astonishment and not without horror.

"I am Tanlu, who loves you and has saved you," he went on. "You are a daughter of the sun, and I do not ask your love in return. I ask only to serve you—"

"You have served me!" she interrupted. "And your life may pay the forfeit! You have slain the prince of the Red Pueblo—you are an outcast—you have broken the law by entering the pueblo here! Oh, fly! Fly before they know and seize you! I would not have you executed now! Fly before they find out, and come for you—"

"Do you not understand, Dezla of the sun? No man may touch me! I am an outcast no longer! The sun priest has made me a man. My brows bear his mark—I have been given sanctuary!"

"It was a trick!" she cried.

"Nevertheless, the marks are upon my brow. I am of the temple! The man who raises his hand against me except in time of war incurs the wrath of the god! All men are sworn to protect me! I have been given sanctuary! Tanlu, the outcast, has been given sanctuary. Do you not understand?"

She looked down into his face and her heart beat faster. The bright moonlight showed that he was smiling at her, and in his face she read what she never before had read in the face of another man.

"It was very clever," she said. "And I am glad! But they will be furious if they learn. You must not tell them!"

"Why not? No man dare touch me! I am not an outcast now, but a man of the temple! And I can be near thee!"

"You have done this—to be near me?"

"I have slain Lazzano to serve thee. I have tricked sanctuary from the priest to be near thee. I love thee. Dezla of the sun, though my love be hopeless!"

"It seems that once I heard the story that Tanlu was of noble birth."

"He is, O Dezla! His father was one of the headmen of the pueblo. But others were jealous of the father and made an outcast of the son!"

"Then thou hast the right to love, since no longer art thou outcast, Tanlu."

"You mean—"

"Dezla means that her heart Is yet her own, a thing to be won. And perhaps under sanctuary Tanlu may do things that will endear him to the hearts of men. And as the sun god comes each morning to brighten the world with his brilliance, so does hope spring daily in the breast of man to urge him to greater things."

"Thy words are like honey, O Dezla!"

"Yet it is best that you guard your name, Tanlu. It were not time yet to sound it before all when thy sanctuary is new and thy deed fresh in the minds of men. I remain thy secret friend. None other knows thy identity!"

She got up and started toward the apartment of the maidens. And she gave a little cry and reeled backward, for she had seen a shadow creep from behind one of the great pillars.

Tanlu whirled on one heel, reaching for his bow, though this was the temple.

The shadow slipped across the stone floor, and passed through a streak of moonlight, and so issued from the temple door. Dezla knew it was the shadow of a man, and she recognized the man as Bruxoli, the watcher. And she knew that the watcher had heard.

• • •

Radzec, cacique of the Red Pueblo, paced the veranda before his house, looking now down at the shelf below which teemed with his subjects, now, at the temple from which came the rhythmic and melancholy tones of the skin-gong that announced the passing of his son.

Radzec pretended a sorrow he did not feel, for Lazzano had been no true son to him.

Lazzano had defied his father on many occasions, and had done little to prepare himself to be cacique in his turn. Little of politics had he understood, and the affair of his marriage, though arranged because of politics, happened to meet the wish of the prince.

Lazzano had first seen Dezla of the sun during a

feast day when he was a visitor at her father's pueblo. He had become stricken with her beauty.

"If you wish me to join you in politics, arrange a marriage with me for Dezla," he had told his father, sneering. "It will cement the two pueblos together against all other foes."

His father had consented gladly, and the match had been arranged. And Lazzano had taken his escort and gone for his bride; and now a runner had come with the news that Lazzano and his escort had been slain on the trail by Tanlu, the outcast, almost within sight of his journey's end.

So Radzec grieved, not so much because of his son's untimely death as over the fact that he had hoped through this marriage to lay claim to the district of the other pueblo when the old cacique died, and thus become a greater lord, and have an army with which he could deal with the ferocious bands that came from the southwest.

The sun was high in the heavens, and on the shelf below the people stopped to worship, offering prayers to the sun god for the rest of the dead prince in the future land.

RADZEC stopped too, and bowed his head, for the cacique did not need to bend a knee except upon special occasions. And then he arose and looked toward the east, and in the distance he saw specks on the trail, and knew that the funeral cortege was near.

Already the watcher of the Red Pueblo had given the signal.

It was an hour before the funeral party entered the pueblo, and during that time Radzec continued his pacing, and once the priest came, up from the temple to comfort him, knowing the truth of matters, for the priest was as hypocritical as the cacique.

Then Radzec could hear the distant chanting, and the people on the shelf below wailed, and the cortege approached. First came 20 young men of noble blood, led by one headman who bent beneath the weight of years. Then came the dead body of the prince, borne by eight young men who had been his familiars.

They reached the shelf and made their way toward the house of the cacique, and stopped at the wall, the people crowding behind them. Radzec drew a deep breath and walked across to meet them.

The old headman bowed low before the cacique, and then bent forward and lifted a skin, and those near could see the dead face of Lazzano, the lips curled back by the agony of violent death.

"My lord, here lies your son," the old headman said. "Here lies Prince Lazzano, whose body we found on the trail within an hour's run of the pueblo to the east, surrounded by the dead bodies of his escort, where all had been done to death most foully."

"Say on!" Radzec commanded.

"He was struck down by a cowardly blow, not

having the chance to fight for his life, for the arrow had entered his back, and well we know Lazzano never would have turned his back knowingly to a foe. He had been in advance of his men, eager perchance to hurry forward and claim his bride. He looked for naught except love and happiness—and he found death. And his death came through treachery."

"What say you? Treachery?" Radzec cried. "Did not Tanlu, the outcast, slay him?"

"Yes, my lord cacique! Tanlu. the outcast, sped the arrow that took the life of the prince. But who shall say what voice urged Tanlu to do the slaying?"

"I would have your meaning," Radzec said.

"I sent spies into the pueblo to the east, my lord, to learn of conditions there. And they tell a peculiar story,"

"Tell it me!"

"After the prince and his escort had been slain, this Tanlu himself carried the news to their pueblo. He pretended before the multitude that he had been of the prince's escort, but the cacique and sun priest evidently knew the- truth. Not only did they not punish with death the outcast who had dared enter a pueblo, but the priest put the marks on his forehead and gave him sanctuary—"

"Gave sanctuary to an outcast who had murdered my son?" Radzec cried.

"Even so, my lord. Washed him clean of blame,

removed the stigma of outcast, gave him sanctuary, made him a man of the temple against whom none other may raise a hand except in war!"

"Now, by the august and brilliant sun—" Radzec began, -but he ceased the oath and motioned for the headman to continue his tale.

"Also, it is whispered in the pueblo, my lord, that Dezla, the daughter of the sun, grieves not because of your son's death. It is said that she did not desire him for husband, and would have refused his suit had not her father urged her to accept it. She is happy, it is said, because he met with this foul death and so could not claim her as his bride. One of the spies made bold to enter the temple when the sun priest was at meat, and he saw a sight that confirms the treachery, my lord."

"What did the man see?"

"Dezla, the daughter of the sun, was in close conversation with this Tanlu, the man who slew your son. They acted as a man and woman who know love. Bruxoli, the watcher, and well known in the pueblo. was in the temple also, and seemed to be guarding them as they spoke. So I say that there has been treachery, my lord, and that it was conspired between those of the pueblo and the outcast that this Tanlu was to slay the prince, and as a reward was to be given sanctuary and made a man again!"

The headman ceased speaking and stepped back, and from the throng there came a murmur, and the murmur grew into a rumbling such as is made by an angry mob. Men branded their spears and shook their bows towards the heavens as they shouted:

"War! War!"

"Lead us, great cacique!"

"Let us avenge thy son!"

But Radzec held up a hand for silence, and the priest of the temple stood beside him and commanded quiet also, and the mob ceased to shout and awaited their cacique's words.

"There is much truth in what you have told me?" he asked the headman.

"It all is truth, my lord. I have the spies here with me."

"And this daughter of the sun held converse with the prince's slayer, you say?"

"Spoke with him in tender tones, my lord, while smiles played over her face where there should have been tearstains because her betrothed had been slain."

"And this Tanlu has been given sanctuary? Their priest dared to do such a thing?"

"He dared!"

Radzec turned away for a moment, and walked a short distance along the wall, while the sun priest stood like a statue and looked out over the people. The cacique reached his spear and picked it up—a gorgeous spear tipped with gold and set with precious stones, a pretty thing not intended for bloody uses. He walked back beside his son's body, and looked down upon it. And he thought not of his son's violent death, but of the fact that here was something that had aroused his people, and that he now could have an excuse to make war, and by conquering add another pueblo to his empire.

He faced the throng for a moment, while they awaited his word, and then he lifted the spear, slowly at first, and suddenly he thrust it upward as far as he could and shook it toward the sun.

"Let there be war?" he said.

Below him the men cheered and brandished their spears. But once more Radzec held up his hand for silence, and the tumult died.

"First, there is a thing of honor to do." he said. "Headman, you will have the body of my son borne into the temple, that we may ask the god to give him peace and happiness in the newer world. And we will go there and listen to the words of the priest."

The young -men picked up the body and continued toward the temple, and the weeping people followed, while Radzec turned aside to the priest and walked alone with him.

"You will know how to speak," he whispered.

"My words shall please you, my lord," the priest replied.

They entered the temple by a little side door, and the priest went up the steps to the altar, before which the body had been placed. The sun came through the opening in the roof and touched the face of the corpse, and the people cried aloud. It was an omen.

And then the sun priest threw wide his arms, and there was immediate silence, and he began to speak.

He knew well what it was that the cacique wanted. There was to be a small eulogy for the prince, one in which his good deeds were magnified and no mention made of his ill ones; but most of all was the priest to make appear loathsome the manner of the prince's death, that the people might thirst for vengeance, and the warriors fight with twice their usual skill and valor.

They were to be made mad with the blood lust, so that they would tear that other eastern pueblo to the ground, and slay all the men and male children, and take what women they willed. They were to ruin a tribe, that Radzec might hold dominion over more land, and people the pueblo anew with his own followers, and put one of his blood in the cacique's place.

The priest began speaking in a low, soft voice, and those below him swayed with his words. And then his tone increased in pitch and grew hysterical, and he urged the warriors to mad deeds in vengeance for the death of the prince. He ended with a fiery peroration that caused the vault of the temple to ring with savage shouts, a wild, barbaric clamor of vengeful anticipation.

The body of the prince was carried to the apartment that was to be his tomb. The people went out of the temple and down the steps, the women to their quarters to prepare a meal and cook food for the warriors to take with them, the men to the great fires that had been built.

"War! War!" they cried. "Vengeance on those who slew the prince! War! To war!"

The arrow-makers worked frantically, urged on by the warriors who clamored for the products of their skill. Men pounded the heads of spears until they were passing sharp. Skins were bound upon shields and body-dress. Flint knives were sharpened. Hatchets were given more weight by rocks fastened to their heads.

Radzec looked from an opening in the side of his house and beheld the scene. He noticed that the men scarcely ate their food, and knew that the blood lust had claimed them. He saw some of them already painting their faces, which meant that they were ready.

## CHAPTER IV

**S**PIES had been sent out along the desert trails. The reflection of the fires could be seen for miles, and the outcasts in the open country guessed that Radzec was about to make war, and wondered where he would strike. And spies from the open country invaded the pueblo to learn, disregarding the law that threatened them with death if they were taken. They got the story, and hastened away to spread it.

League after league it travelled, until it reached a goatherd who lived near the pueblo to the east. He was no outcast, save such as his profession made him. He could come and go in the pueblo at will.

Night had come by the time the goatherd got the news, and the fires of the Red Pueblo were so far away that their reflection could not be seen there, nor from the top of the lookout rock. But the goatherd knew through what channel the intelligence had arrived; knew that it could be trusted.

He nodded a brief farewell to the woman who shared his forlorn existence, picked up his crooked staff, and went out along the trail. He was not an old man, yet he could not travel fast, and it was some distance to the pueblo.

He hurried along the trail, going as swiftly as he could, kicking up great clouds of dust behind him, crunching cacti beneath his sandalled feet. He had heard it said that the night watcher at the pueblo had eyes almost as good as those of Bruxoli, and was thankful that the moon was not shining this night.

For he did not wish to enter the pueblo openly and cry his news for all to hear. He had other methods in mind. Now and then he stopped to listen, fearful that some wandering guard might come across him, but he heard nobody. And after a time he came to where he could see the watch-fire of the pueblo.

The goatherd was more cautious now. He dodged from shadow to shadow, stopped to listen, approached the edge of the pueblo a pace at a time.

He circled in such manner that there was a great rock between himself and the fire, and so its light did not reach him. He evaded two guards at the mouth of the trail, and found himself inside their lines. But he had yet to make the long climb to the first shelf, and the ladders always were guarded.

Only a goatherd who had followed his flocks
through the rough hills could have done what he did
then. He started up the face of the cliff, holding to
little projections that were scarcely large enough to
furnish resting-place for foot or hand. It was a difficult climb, and tiring, but the goatherd did not hesitate.

Near the shelf he paused when he heard a guard
walking along above him. He waited until the warrior had passed, and then drew himself up carefully,.
keeping in the shadows, and so gained the smooth
space. He darted to one side, against the face of a
community house. And then he began creeping,
crouching, down the shelf toward the temple.

There was a space to be crossed where the light of
the fire penetrated, and at the edge of it the goatherd paused to pull a skin over his head so that he
would not be recognized readily if any man saw
him.

He walked across the light space with a regular
gait, like a man not in hiding, and gained the shadows on the other side without having been seen by a
guard.

Now he faced the steps before the temple entrance, and after hesitating a moment to listen he
hurried up them like a ghost, making not the slightest sound. At the temple entrance he paused again,
for he had not the right to enter at this hour, and did
the priest happen to be awake and seize him, he

might receive punishment.

Then he drew a deep breath and entered, and presently stood in the big room with its arched root and its opening through which the sun poured his blessings.

Word had travelled into the open country that day how Tanlu had been granted sanctuary and how none in the pueblo knew his true identity, and the goatherd had received it and passed it on. He knew, now, that Tanlu, the outcast, was somewhere in the temple.

Yet he could not make a disastrous mistake, for the quarters of the sun-maidens were indicated plainly, and an underpriest stalked back and forth before the door, on guard. He had only to search on the other side of the altar-room, in the little apartments there.

Careful that the guard did not see him, he slipped behind the skin curtains of the first room and stood still to listen. To his ears there came the regular breathing of a man. The goatherd wished for the moon now, that its beams would enter the room and show him the face of the sleeper, but the moon was hiding behind the clouds that hung low on the horizon.

He slipped closer to the sleeping man, and bent over him. His presence gave a warning to the slumberer, who sat up quickly on his bed of skins.

"What is the name of the man who disturbs my

rest?" he demanded.

Joy sang in the heart of the goatherd, for the voice was that of Tanlu.

"Tanlu! Master!" he hissed. "It is the goatherd, Bezo by name."

"What do you here, fellow?"

"I bring news."

"You bring a stench, also, by the gods!"

"Peace, master! I have crossed the open country and hurried to you, slipping in past the guards and searching for you in the temple at this hour."

"Thy news?"

"The Red Pueblo is aroused. The body of the prince was taken home for burial. In the cortege were spies who had been visiting the pueblo here. They reported that you slew Lazzano, and were given sanctuary for the deed. It is believed the people here had it arranged with you. They said, also, that Dezla, the daughter of the sun, loved not the prince of the Red Pueblo, and so had you slay him, and that as a reward she will give her love to you."

"I wish it were true! Say on!"

"Even now at the Red Pueblo the great fires are burning, and the warriors are sharpening their spears and making arrows. Radzec has held his jewelled spear aloft—and it is to be war!"

"War!" Tanlu asked. "They are to make war on these people here?"

"They think the death of the prince was planned

because the daughter of the sun did not wish him for a husband, and that you were rewarded with sanctuary for the deed. They will march at dawn, perhaps, every warrior Radzec can muster. Two nights from now they will arrive and attack while the pueblo sleeps. Their priest of the sun made a speech and urged them to leave not a single male among the living."

"You have done well to bring me this news before telling it to others." Tanlu said. "None here except the daughter of the sun knows that I am Tanlu, the outcast."

"And what shall I do now, my master?"

Tanlu got up and paced the stone floor while he thought, and after a time he sat down on his bed of skins again.

"You will slip from the pueblo." he directed, "and regain the open country. Then you will return, and this time you will let the guards see you. You will cry your news for all to hear, give the alarm, say that the intelligence came to you on the desert through the outcasts."

"I go, my master! You—you are safe here?"

"Were I not, could a goatherd do much toward proving my safety?" Tanlu observed the other with the flicker of a smile, for a moment a something almost regal in his poise.

"Pardon, master! I did but fear for you. You have been so good to us."

"You have my pardon—and my thanks. Go!"

## CHAPTER V

DEZO, the goatherd, made haste from the temple, for he knew that it was near the dawn, and he did not want the sharp eyes of the watcher to observe him leaving the pueblo and entering it again.

He hurried down the long flight of steps and crept along the shelf, and when the nearest guards had their backs turned he let himself over the edge and began the perilous descent.

Descending was not so easy as climbing. yet he accomplished it without disaster, and crawled from rock to rock until he was in the dense darkness. Safe from the sight of the guards, he went as swiftly as he could in a great circle until he struck the trail, and down that he hurried for some distance, and finally stopped to rest near a clump of brush.

The goatherd was a man more devout than many

in the pueblos, for he generally greeted the dawn, and knelt facing the rising sun to ask blessings of the brilliant god. No watcher on a lookout rock gave a signal that caused a gong to be struck out in the ragged hills where he tended his flock.

And now he sat facing the east, sat upon his heels, and waited for the first pink streak to come in the sky. And when it came he bent forward eagerly, watching the rim of the mountains, seeing the pink glow turn into red, and then into orange. And then the edge of the brilliant orb showed, over the rim, and the goatherd gazed in ecstasy, and bowed thrice rapidly, and then looked up to find the eye of the god upon him.

"Master of all light!" he cried. "Just and august deity! Grant, I beseech, that my friend, Tanlu, the outcast, come with honor and all his skin through this sorry business!"

He sprang to his feet then, and picked up his crooked staff, and started along the trail toward the pueblo, going as swiftly as he could, and knowing that the eyes of the watcher already were upon him.

He could see the form of Bruxoli against the brightening sky at the top of the rock, and he began waving his arms in the manner of a man trying to attract attention and give an alarm.

Bruxoli saw him, and signalled to those below. First he held up a hand to show that one came along the trail, and then he extended his arms and whirled on one foot to indicate trouble, and then he flapped his hands at his sides much as a rooster flaps his wings before it crows, which meant that the one approaching was making speed and evidently needed help.

So the gong on the roof of the temple struck, and some of the guards ran down the ladders, spears in readiness, to greet the newcomer. Bezo, the goatherd, ran up to them, gasping and panting and seemingly unable to get breath enough for speech.

"The cacique! Take me to the cacique!" he cried. "I have news!"

"The ladder is before you," one of the guards said.

Bezo hurried up the ladder, making it rock with his ascent. At the top more guards would have stopped him, but he begged to be sent straightway into the presence of the cacique, or the sun-priest.

"The men of the Red Pueblo are coming!" Bezo shouted; and then he ran on to the house of the cacique.

The guards before the doorway stopped him, and once more he repeated that he had news, and the old cacique heard the tumult and came to the door to see what might be its cause.

"What is thy news, foul one? Thy intelligence, keeper of goats?" he demanded.

"The news came to me through the desert and its people. O cacique!" Bezo cried. "I have run from my

poor hut to warn thee. The people of the Red
Pueblo even now prepare for war against thee and
thine. Their fires are burning, and their warriors are
sharpening their spears."

"What is this?" the cacique cried.

The bronze of his old face had turned to white,
for this was the thing that he had feared for years.
He loved peace and he knew that his men were not
ready for war, nor did they have a proper leader.

"It is the sad truth, O cacique!" Bezo went on.
"The body of the Prince Lazzano was borne to his
father, and because of that there is to be war."

"Why because of that, fellow?"

"Because Tanlu slew the prince, the cacique of
the Red Pueblo will come and slay your warriors,
and wreck your houses and drive away your
women."

"Are we responsible for the acts of Tanlu, the outcast?"

"The people of the Red Pueblo say so, my lord!"

The shelf was filled with people now, and the
priest was pushing his way through the crowd, and
all heard the goatherd's words.

"Am I to blame because Lazzano died?" the cacique asked.

"So says the terrible Radzec, my lord. It was a
plot, he says. His spies have carried him the intelligence. They have told that Dezla, the daughter of
the sun, did not wish to mate with Lazzano, and that

you plotted with Tanlu to slay him so that the wedding could not be."

"A foolish thought!"

"But events have given it substance, my lord, and I pray you believe in the truth of my words, and prepare. They say that after he had slain the prince, Tanlu, the outcast, himself carried the news to your pueblo, and that as a reward the sun-priest marked his brow and gave him sanctuary."

"How is this?" the cacique cried. "What nonsense is this? Gave sanctuary to Tanlu, the outcast?"

"And they have said that thy daughter, Dezla, looks with love into the eyes of Tanlu, which is another reason why Tanlu, slew the prince."

"Dog!" the cacique cried. "Dare you repeat such a slander? Have your wits grown as crooked as the staff you carry?"

"That is what the spies reported to Radzec, my lord."

"Those things are not to be believed!"

"Yet because of them the warriors of the Red Pueblo are sharpening their weapons and painting their faces. They now are on the trail. In two nights they will attack."

"It is not to be believed! It is a trick of this Radzec!" cried the cacique. "We gave sanctuary to none but one of the prince's escort, who fetched news of his death."

Now the man of whom he spoke came walking

slowly down the steps of the temple. and he stopped a few steps from the bottom, as if wondering at the commotion. The sun-priest and the cacique hurried across to his side.

"Who art thou?" the cacique demanded.

"Does it matter?"

"It matters much, if this goatherd's tale be true. You did tell us that you were one of the Prince Lazzano's escort—"

"Your pardon, my lord! If you will remember my words correctly, you will recollect that I said no such thing. Perchance you took that to be my meaning."

His eyes were twinkling, and he came down another step.

"Thy name?" the cacique demanded.

"I have been called Tanlu."

A GASP of horror came from the crowd. The sun priest had a brow like thunder. The old cacique was white of face again.

"Tanlu, the outcast?" he cried.

"No longer, my lord. Tanlu, sealed of the sanctuary. Tanlu, the man! I bear the mark upon my brow, and even you, noble cacique. dare not efface It!"

"You got it by a trick!"

"Still, I have it! I was tired of being an outcast in the desert. I grew tired of hearing blamed to me the oppressions and transgressions of other men. I am of noble birth. I did but use my brain to claim my rightful place in the world of men."

"You have the blood of the Prince Lazzano upon your hands!"

"I have, and glory in it, cacique. For I have saved a maiden from much misery. The daughter of the sun had no love for the man you would have given her to. And in your own heart you were sorrowful at such a thing, yet you agreed because you feared the cacique of the Red Pueblo."

"You have tricked us—and now the Red Pueblo warriors are coming against us! They will slay our men and wreck our homes and carry away our women!"

Now the throng surged forward, shrieking at him because of their fear and anger, the men brandishing their spears.

"Kill the outcast!" they cried. "He has dared visit a pueblo! Slay the outcast, the man who has brought war upon us!"

Tanlu sprang up a step as they rushed toward him, and swept his spear before him and held it ready.

"Stop!" he cried. "I have been given sanctuary, but if there is one among you courageous enough to face me, I will call it war, and the sanctuary will not hold! Let the courageous one speak know!"

He looked down upon them, and they quailed before his glance, and his lips formed in a sneer.

"Is this thy courage?" he cried. "Are you mere

children playing with spears and arrows? Could you be men if an insult was passed? I do not wonder, O cacique, that you fear the fight that is coming, if these be thy best men!"

Their angry roar answered him, and they charged at him again.

"Back!" he cried. "Let any two of you step forward and face me. You hang back? What manner of men are you? Will you fight, or shall you let the Red Pueblo warriors work their will?"

A man fitted an arrow to bow, but the sun priest hurled him aside.

"Are you mad? The man has sanctuary!" he cried.

"He has betrayed us!" shrieked the old cacique. "Perhaps he is in league with the Red Pueblo himself!"

That was another thought for the mob. Again they surged forward, shrieking their maledictions at him, shaking their fists, brandishing their weapons.

And then the daughter of the sun came through the temple door and ran speedily down the stone steps. She stopped in front of Tanlu, and faced the throng; and they suddenly were quiet and respectful, for they loved her.

"Oh, men of little sense!" she cried. "Are you babes that you quarrel among yourselves and with one who would save you? Have you forgotten the god that you would touch a man who has sanctuary?"

"He has betrayed us!" a voice cried.

"He has served me, my people. Because we are not strong, my father was forced to promise me as bride to a man I could neither love nor respect. And this Tanlu killed him, to save me from sorrow and misery. Suppose he did gain sanctuary by a trick. At the same time he gained his proper standing among men. He was made outcast when he should have been honored. He has lived a good life. He has not done half the things with which you blame him. He told me so—and I believe!"

"He has brought war upon us!"

"Fools! Was it his doing? The cacique of the Red Pueblo but waited for an excuse to make war. He knows we are weak. But we are not cowards! Sharpen your spears. Make your arrows. Paint your faces. Pile fuel on the war fires and gather your courage. Meet the warriors of the Red Pueblo face to face, and beat them back!"

"It cannot be done!" the old cacique cried. "I have no son! We have no general! Where is the man to lead us?"

Tanlu stepped out before them.

"I am the man!" he said simply.

"Thou?" the cacique cried.

"I paint out the mark of sanctuary and become the warrior, O cacique! Is my arm not strong? Is there a man of the pueblo who dares stand before me? Have I not won my name as a killer of men? I

have spent these years in the open country, an outcast, and every trail and hiding-place is known to
me!

"I can find water for an army where another
army would die of thirst. I can find food in the
midst of the desert. I have visited pueblos when it
was death to be caught, and have learned many
things. I know the weakness of every one. And I hate
Radzec, the cacique of the Red Pueblo, and swear to
have his head, if you will have me for leader!"

There was quiet for a moment, for such a thing
never had been heard of before. The old cacique
looked at this man on the temple steps, and caught
himself wishing that he had such a son. The sun
priest frowned and said nothing.

"We are few in numbers," the cacique mumbled,
then.

"You are few in numbers, true," Tanlu cried. "But
there are allies."

"That is so. But the pueblo where our allies live is
six days' run to the south. Radzec shall have beaten
us before they could give us aid."

"There are other allies, If you have me for
leader!" Tanlu cried. "I am beloved in the open
country. Ask Bezo the goatherd here. I have but to
lift my voice. and they will rally to the cry of Tanlu!"

"That is true, O cacique!" the goatherd cried.

"There are hundreds of them, cacique—fierce,
untamed men whose bosoms are torn with sorrow

and suffering. Radzec of the Red Pueblo put the mark of the outcast on the most, because of little things of no importance, and on many because Lazzano, his profligate son, asked it Think you that they will therefore fight beside you against the warriors of the Red Pueblo? Give them the chance. O cacique. Let me but send this honest, though evil-smelling goatherd out into the open country with word for them to gather here with their weapons. Before the night falls again they will begin coming if I am to lead them!"

"And thy reward, if you do this thing and we are victorious?" the old cacique asked, with something of fear in his manner.

"Only that my noble blood be recognized and all stigma removed from my name, and that I be allowed to sit at meat with thy best men!" Tanlu said.

Dezla hung her head quickly when she heard the words, for she knew well their full meaning. Recognized as of noble blood, and allowed to sit at meat with the warriors, Tanlu could claim what he could win—even the heart of the daughter of the sun.

"Your demands are modest and smack of honesty," the old cacique was saying. "You may lead us, Tanlu!"

## CHAPTER VI

FOR a moment there was silence while the full meaning of his words sank into their minds, and then from men, women, and children there came a chorus of cries that approved of the cacique's decision, for the people had been stricken with fear, and here was something that promised them aid.

But those of noble blood did not cheer, and there were black looks on their bronze faces, and they turned their backs upon Tanlu and spoke together in whispers. Presently they began to drift through the throng and away one by one, and after a time they gathered again in the house of one Sazzac at the far end of the shelf.

Sazzac was a man of wealth, and his ancestors had been great in wars and had handed him down a name which he found considerable difficulty to maintain. Because of his wealth he was able to purchase popularity, for he had goats to give to the hungry and precious jewels to present to his friends.

The walls of his house were decorated with drawings and carvings that told of the prowess of his ancestors, and before these pictures his guests bowed this morning as they entered, for it was the custom.

Sazzac clapped his hands and a slave entered to receive orders, and soon the other nobles were served with food and drink. And while they ate and drank Sazzac looked them over, and speculated concerning them and what he was about to attempt. Not a man in the house but was under obligations to him.

After a time he motioned for a slave to stand at the door and give the alarm if anyone approached, and then he sat down at the head of the big room and faced the others.

"The brilliant god has seen fit to make our plans come to naught." he said.

"Not so, oh, Sazzac!" one cried. "In such affairs the god favors neither side, but urges to the test and then smiles upon the victor. Our plans have been ruined by a man."

"Then there is sore need of new arrangements," Sazzac said; "and what is to be done must be done quickly. Has anyone a thought, or must I speak?"

"Speak, Sazzac!" they cried in chorus, knowing well that he wished to do so.

"There is an oath of blood brotherhood amongst us." he said. "We have sworn to accomplish an end, and there are no traitors amongst us."

He glanced at them, and every man met his eyes squarely.

"We have fallen upon evil days in this our pueblo," he continued. "Our cacique has no son, and the years grow heavy upon him. As a people, we are growing weaker, and soon we shall be the prey of all parasites of the open country. Where is our dignity, our prestige, our pride? They are gone because of lack of leadership.

"True, Sazzac!" they cried.

"Soon the old cacique must go the way of his fathers, and then we shall be left without a head. Some time ago we considered these things and evolved a plan. I am of the best blood among you, and it was decided that I should be cacique when our old master dies, and you swore to uphold my hands in that business."

"True, oh, Sazzac!"

"It was decided, also, that I take Dezla, the daughter of the sun, for my bride, because she is of royal blood and should have a cacique or prince for a husband. And then we were told that the cacique had promised her to the Prince Lazzano, of the Red Pueblo. We knew what that meant. It meant that, after our cacique's death, this Lazzano would come to rule us for his father, and we of the best blood would be made to kiss the feet of the Red Pueblo's nobles. So we decided upon a plan for the betterment of our community."

He stopped and looked at the slave who stood near the door, but the slave motioned that no one come near to listen.

"We decided to slay this Lazzano as he was about to enter the temple to claim his bride, to declare that the old cacique was deposed and that I ruled in his stead, and I was to go into the temple in this Lazzano's place, and force Dezla to wed me. Then we were to send word to our allies to the south to come and aid us, and notify the cacique of the Red Pueblo of what we had done, and dare him to attack us."

"True, oh, Sazzac!" they cried.

"And now we are undone. This Tanlu, the outcast, slays the prince on a desert trail, and comes here and gains sanctuary, and we are faced with war and yet have not accomplished our ends. And now he has been made to lead us! We are nobles, and shall we submit to be led by this outcast man who has been living with the rats of the desert? Shall we take his commands, and carry them out?"

They snarled by way of reply, for all in the room were jealous that Tanlu had been named to lead them, and hated him for the favor he had received at the hands of the cacique.

"We must have a new plan, and at once," Sazzac went on. "Do I hear a thought?"

None spoke, and for a time he bent his head in his hands and remained thus, thinking.

"You are my true friends?" he asked, after a time.

"We are, Sazzac!" they cried.

"And are willing to stand at my back? It is good! Then we must go to the cacique and in the presence of the sun priest tell him that we will not go to war behind this Tanlu, because it is not proper for men of noble blood to be led by one who has been an outcast and would be one yet but for a trick!"

"We will go!" they cried.

"If the cacique does not uphold us, then will we depose him, and I shall declare myself cacique in his place. And I shall wed Dezla, and you who are my friends shall have added wealth and honors."

They shouted his name now, thrusting their spears above their heads.

Yet one of his friends made bold to speak.

"What this Tanlu said was true in part. He knows the secrets of the open country, where to find water and food, and he has been living by his wits and therefore is a shrewd man in some things. I doubt not he has clever plans for this warfare. Let us not say a word to the cacique until the morrow, and meanwhile let us listen to this Tanlu while he plans. Let him do the work of organization this day, and when we depose the cacique tomorrow we will know what this Tanlu has planned. Then we can make the war without him, using the arrangements he has made, and the greater glory will be ours when we have been victorious. The name of Sazzac will be one to strike terror to his foes, and it will be an excellent joke on this Tanlu."

"Thou hast a head on thy shoulders!" Sazzac cried. "I shall present you with a jewelled spear. But it comes to my mind that this Tanlu has sent into the open country for the outcasts to be our allies!"

"Fear not because of them. Sazzac. They probably will camp outside the pueblo, waiting for the war. It is death for them to enter, for so says the law. It may be necessary that we slay this Tanlu when the cacique is deposed, and afterward certain of us can go among the outcasts as their captains saying that Tanlu sent us, and in the fighting they will not know but what Tanlu is the general. After the victory we can drive them into the desert again."

"It is well," Sazzac said, "let us keep counsel for this day, then. and tomorrow when the sunrise gong strikes we will go to the cacique and make known our will to him!"

They left the house of Sazzac one and two at a time, so as not to attract attention, and mingled with the crowd; and after a time Sazzac himself walked along the shelf, attended by half a dozen slaves, some of whom carried his spear and bow and arrows. Sazzac appeared the great chieftain, and common folk crept out of his path

The big fires had been kindled, and the smoke

signals poured upward toward the sky. Warriors chanted as they ground the heads of their spears, the arrow-makers were busy, and the old men who could fight no longer sat in circles and told tales of earlier days when they had been in their prime and their enemies feared them.

Sazzac walked toward the house of the cacique, where Tanlu was talking to some of the headmen, and the other nobles in the conspiracy met him there, one at a time. And when they could, without causing comment, they asked for a council of war, and entered the cacique's house to hold it.

"Tanlu, our new leader, is wise to the ways of the desert," Sazzac said. "He knows the secrets that may make an army successful in its campaign. No doubt he has plans for the war that is coming. But what if the brilliant god in his wisdom takes Tanlu from us during the early hours of the strife?"

"What means Sazzac?" the cacique asked.

"Were this to be regretted thing to occur, we would be beaten," Sazzac went on. "For our enemies would find us with plans partially carried out, and no man knows how to continue. It has occurred to me that this Tanlu, our new and valorous leader, should take some of the noble chieftains into his confidence regarding his plans, so, should he die on an enemy's spear, our cause would not fail."

"That is an excellent thought," the cacique said.

"It is." Tanlu agreed.

"I suggest, O cacique," Sazzac went on, "that this Tanlu take certain ones of us to the crest of the lookout rock, and there point over the desert and tell us some of his secrets."

"It is well," Tanlu said.

The cacique bowed his permission, and Tanlu led the way along the upper shelf to the narrow ladder, the nobles following behind him, Sazzac in the lead. Their faces did not betray their glee at the success of their stratagem.

They made the perilous climb leaving all their weapons at the bottom of the ladder as the law said, and finally reached the summit of the rock, to find Bruxoli, the watcher, on duty there. He turned and gave them a single glance, answered their respectful salutes, and faced toward the west again.

Tanlu took his place a short distance from the watcher, and pointed toward the south. He showed where armed men might hide in such manner that they could swoop down upon an enemy. He showed where men in retreat might find water and food while their enemy starved, not knowing the secrets of the open country. He revealed to them where guards should be placed, and he gave them a plan of campaign.

And all the time their ears were wide to catch this intelligence, and all the time the watcher went about his business of gazing over the world below as if there had been no human being near him on the rock.

Sazzac looked into the eyes of his friends, and messages flashed between them, and they rejoiced at the stupidity of this Tanlu, who put his plans into their hands, so that they might kill him and yet not suffer because of the loss of his generalship.

When Tanlu had finished, they asked certain questions, and when all had been answered they descended the long ladder again. Tanlu waiting to be last. And just as he turned to set foot upon the first rung, the watcher darted from the top of the rock and touched him on the arm.

"A word, Tanlu!" he said.

"Tanlu knows the word you would speak, faithful man. and he answers that all will be well."

"The daughter of the sun—"

"Has my right arm to guard her if it prove necessary. 1 will not forget that I am of noble blood. I am no outcast to commit crimes, but a man of honor again because of the mark on my brow."

"It is well," the watcher said. "My heart burns for love of the daughter of the sun. Because of my lowly birth she may not be my wife, yet may 1 serve her."

"Yet you may! She has a loyal friend in the watcher."

"So long as you proceed with honor, Tanlu, I shall be at your back in all things."

"I thank you, Bruxoli."

The watcher was pleased that Tanlu called him

by his name, for that was an honor from one of no-ble birth.

"There are things—" he began.

"Tanlu knows all things!"

"It is well," Bruxoli said; and he hurried back to the crest of the rock.

Tanlu went down the long ladder.

Bezo, the goatherd, had done his work well. Just after the midday gong had struck the watcher sig-nalled that persons approached along the trail, and the guards hurried down the ladders. Nor was it necessary to climb the lockout rock to see them. From all directions they came—bronze men who had lived in the open country, carrying their spears and shields and bows and hatchets, chanting their individual war-songs.

Some ran swiftly along the trails as if the battle already was on, whale others came in bands, and cautiously, realizing that they were still outcasts and that the law said it was death for them to enter a pueblo.

## CHAPTER VII

TANLU went out to meet them, and they brandished their spears and greeted him with shouts. He bade them camp along the watercourse a quarter of a mile from the end of the pueblo, and there they built their fires and cooked their food, which they had brought with them.

Throughout the afternoon they gathered, until they numbered almost as many as the warriors of the pueblo. and throughout the night they continued to come, answering the call of Tanlu, their friend and champion, ready to do battle when he so ordered, eager to clash with the men of the Red Pueblo.

Their fires sprang toward the sky and made light the open country for miles around. And yet they were shrewd, these outcasts, for no spy from the Red Pueblo got near enough to witness the mobilization. On every trail there were guards, and no man was allowed to pass. And so it was reported to Radzec that the war fires were burning in the pueblo to the east, and Radzec laughed boisterously and declared that the men there had heard of his contemplated war, and were attempting to gather the courage they lacked.

When the dawn came, and the great gong of the temple struck, there was a pretty scene down by the water-course, where the hundreds of outcasts knelt facing the rising sun and praised the brilliant god. Up in the pueblo the people crowded the temple—men, women and children—and the sun priest asked the brilliant god to grant victory in the fight that was to come.

Dezla, daughter of the sun, stood up before them on the high steps and added her supplication, and then went among the women trying to comfort them. Tanlu, wearing about his neck the necklace of a general, walked among the warriors, evidently thinking deeply.

The throng disbanded, and the morning meal was prepared, and those of the pueblo ate. More fuel was thrown on the fires, green fuel, so that columns of smoke would rise toward the heavens and call to the allies in the south.

And then Sazzac and the other nobles marched along the ledge to the house of the cacique, and said that they wished important speech with him, and asked that the sun priest and Tanlu be present. They were brave in paint and feathers, and carried their jewelled spears, and slaves behind them held their bows and arrows.

"Speak, Sazzac!" the cacique ordered, when all were assembled.

Sazzac glanced at the other nobles and cleared his throat. He was at a loss how to begin, though he had rehearsed his speech half a hundred times during the night. He looked toward Tanlu, and saw him stern of face and waiting, and hatred rose in his breast.

"Great cacique, your nobles are come with a protest," he said.

"A time of war is no moment to argue about petty things, Sazzac," the cacique said. "In time of war a people must stand together else that people falls!"

"This is no petty thing, O cacique! I am of noble blood, and so are these men who stand at my back."

"That is well known. Say on!"

"We are entitled to the privileges of our positions. And now by thy order, cacique, we are to serve under a man who has been an outcast, and would be yet but for a trick he played."

"Those are bold words!" Tanlu said. He stood with his arms folded across his breast, and his eyes burned into those of Sazzac.

"And true ones!" Sazzac added, while the nobles murmured behind him. "Cacique, we demand that

this man be sent out into the desert where he be-
longs. We of noble blood cannot follow him!"

"How is this?" the cacique cried. "Is not Tanlu of
noble blood?"

"He was at birth, but that blood has been tainted
because he has been an outcast!"

"Beware!" Tanlu cried. "Speak softer words, or
you will feel the point of my spear."

"We demand that this man be dismissed, cacique!" Sazzac went on, ignoring Tanlu.

"Where then will we have a man to lead us?" the
cacique asked.

"Am I not capable?" Sazzac asked.

"This Tanlu has called his hundreds of friends to
be our allies, and he knows the secrets of the desert!"

"No more so than do we!" Sazzac replied.

"How is this?"

"He has taken us to the summit of the lookout
rock, and there he has explained to us the secrets of
the trails and watering-places. He has explained, too,
his plans of campaign. Since we know his knowledge
we do not need the man!"

"And his friends?"

"Some of us will go down among them as captains, and they will think that they serve under
Tanlu's orders. They will fight the same as though
he led them."

"But I have named this Tanlu leader!" the cacique
protested. "Must not a cacique keep his spoken

word?"

"Not necessarily to a man who has been outcast. Depose him, cacique, and I will lead your armies, and these noble friends of mine shall be my captains. It is not fitting that the men of our pueblo be led by the outcast who brought this awful war upon us."

"Enough of this!" Tanlu cried. "You speak treason! I am leader of these armies and my word is law!"

"We are asking the cacique to depose you!" Sazzac said.

"And so you would take my knowledge and make war with it." Tanlu asked.

"Why not?"

"Because you are slow of wit and I read what was in your minds. And when we went to the summit of the lookout rock, I did but tell you a maze of falsehoods to suit your characters. Follow the instructions I gave you then and your men will be scattered, they will die of hunger and thirst, and the warriors of the Red Pueblo will hunt you down to the last man, and Radzec rule here!"

"It is a lie!" Sazzac thundered.

"It is not a lie! You thought to play with Tanlu, and have been beaten at the game."

SAZZAC'S eyes blazed for a moment, and he realized that Tanlu was speaking the truth. But he was not to be outdone.

"Then let it be so!" he cried. "We do not need your intelligence. We are capable of conducting this war without you! What say you, cacique? Does this man go?"

"Suppose I judge that he should remain our general?" the old cacique said.

Sazzac turned to look at the nobles behind him.

"Cacique, you are an honored man, yet an old one," he said. "Our people have been growing tame because of it. It is fitting that we be a strong people and rule with skill in this pueblo and its neighborhood. We should be so strong that our enemies will fear to attack us. We nobles have come to the conclusion that it were better if a younger man were cacique!"

"What is this?" their old chief cried.

"I have spoken."

"And whom would you name for cacique in my place?"

"The nobles have named myself," Sazzac told him. "Either Tanlu is deposed by your order, else we depose you both!"

The words were spoken. The sun priest stepped forward with an exclamation of horror. but recoiled before Sazzac's blazing eyes. The old cacique looked up at the young noble from a white face.

"So you would cast me out!" he said.

"Do you bid this Tanlu go?"

"No! My word shall remain unbroken!"

"Then must I seize command and have myself declared the cacique of this pueblo!"

"Pause!" Tanlu cried in a loud voice. "Think you that treason can prosper, Sazzac? Think you everyone is blind? Yesterday when you met with these nobles I was within hearing, anticipating that treason would be spoken, for I had read your minds. I overheard all your plans. and that is why 1 gave you false information on the summit of the lookout rock."

"Then our spears must take your life!" Sazzac cried.

Tanlu laughed raucously and stepped backward. Twice he clapped his hands, and around the two ends of the cacique's house rushed rugged men of the open country. Three deep, in a rank 40 men long, they arranged themselves, and looked to Tanlu for command.

"You see, we have been prepared for your treason!" Tanlu said.

"These be outcasts—they have entered the pueblo—the law says they must die!"

"And who shall slay them?" Tanlu demanded. "You and your nobles? Draw your bows, then, and cast your spears! Who shall be the first to do so?"

The nobles knew better than to attempt such a thing.

"So be it!" Sazzac said presently. "We will allow this Tanlu to be our general, O cacique, though we have no hope for success. And when we have been defeated, remember that we warned you!"

"Pause!" Tanlu cried again. "Do you believe you will escape unpunished after speaking treason and attempting to depose your cacique?"

"We are of noble blood!"

"All the greater reason you should be punished."

"And how may we be? You have need of every spear!"

"The spears of traitors are of little account, Sazzac!"

"You would make us outcasts, I suppose?" Sazzac sneered.

'The outcasts of the open country would refuse to receive you among them, Sazzac. They be honest folk!"

"Well, then?"

"You shall be assigned to the outcast bands, and there you shall fight! And men will watch you, to see that you fight properly. If you do not, there will be spears thrust through your backs! That is clear?"

"You would dare?" Sazzac cried. "We have followers!"

"And already they have been scattered among the bands of outcasts, where they are watched and can do no mischief! You stand alone!"

Now Tanlu walked forward until he faced the haughty Sazzac, and with his own hand he reached up and tore the necklace of rank from Sazzac's throat.

Sazzac screeched his rage at the indignity, and the outcasts presented their spears. And then Tanlu tore the badges of rank from the throat of each noble; and ground them beneath his heels, and stepped back.

"You may have back your rank when you have won it," he said. "Be brave and loyal in the fight that is to come, and perhaps you may be forgiven. Go!"

The chief of the nobles hung his head from shame, and turned and walked through the throng, his friends after him. Some of the captains of the outcasts seized upon them and took them away, to scatter them among the several bands.

'Tanlu, thou hast saved me!" the old cacique said.

"I have defeated treason," Tanlu replied.

He turned away and hurried toward the temple. And on the lowest step he met Dezla, the daughter of the sun.

"I have heard, Tanlu," she said. "And I am grateful, for 1 do love my old father much. But beware of Sazzac! He is cunning and cruel. He underestimated thy merit once, but he will not do so again. Beware of Sazzac!"

Along the desert trails Tanlu's spies came running with new intelligence.

Radzec had heard that the pueblo knew of his contemplated attack, and so had delayed one day, that his men might be in better condition for the campaign. He would not reach the pueblo with his forces this night, but upon the night following the next dawn.

Tanlu then hurried to where the outcast bands were camped along the water-course, and he held long conversation with their chiefs. The war drums sounded, and the bands of outcasts gathered their weapons and started away toward the west as Tanlu went back to the temple.

"You have sent the men of the desert away?" the old cacique asked.

"They have marched, and the traitorous nobles are in their midst," Tanlu replied.

"Then the outcasts are not to fight for us, even after we allowed them to disregard the law and enter the pueblo?"

"In deed they sire to fight for us, O cacique! It is all a part of my plan. These outcast bands will circle through the desert, keeping the range of yellow hills between themselves and Radzec's advancing army. The spies will watch, and if there be danger of discovery, the outcasts will so hide themselves that Radzec will pass without being aware of their nearness."

"And how will that benefit?" the cacique asked.

"After Radzec has passed, the outcasts will make all haste to the Red Pueblo. There they will find naught but a few guards and old men, and women and children. They will tear the pueblo rock from

rock, and seize all food and goods of war, all blan-
kets and pottery for their spoils."

"And while they are doing that—"

"While they are doing that, Radzec's army will
besiege this pueblo. We will have the ladders drawn
up, and fight from the shelf. We are strong enough
to hold them off for days, if we battle well."

"And then?" the cacique asked.

"Having finished at the Red Pueblo, the outcasts
will turn back and attack Radzec's forces in the rear,
O cacique. At the same time we shall sally forth, and
between our forces and the outcasts the men of the
Red Pueblo will find death!"

"An admirable general!" the sun priest said; and
he went forward and blessed Tanlu again.

# CHAPTER VIII

TANLU went out and gave orders. and food and water were carried into the pueblo, and the long ladders were drawn up, and the pueblo thus cut off from the world.

Men labored like slaves to carry great rocks and place them in piles along the edge of the shelf, from where they could be hurled down upon the heads of Radzec's warriors. Arrows were piled in places where they could be obtained easily when they were needed, and some of the apertures in the houses were closed.

All day the great fires sent their columns of dense smoke toward the sky. The women cooked food, and spent a great deal of time in the temple praying for the welfare of their men, and the children ran about, shouting in excitement, or else stood to one side out of the way, forefinger in mouth, and wondered at it all.

Tanlu seemed to be everywhere shouting his orders and preparing for the battle that was to come, and men learned that day to trust him and to admire his cunning. He had painted out the marks of sanctuary on his brow for the time being, and had streaked his face with red and purple, which showed that he was at war and also was a great chieftain in his tribe.

And then the night came, and Bruxoli the watcher descended from his rock and let the night man take his place, and those of the pueblo ate their fill and a little more, for Tanlu had ordered that after this night there should be eaten as little as possible. He knew that food was the thing most needed during a siege, unless it be water.

Through the early hours of the night the men continued working, and then they stretched themselves for a long and heavy sleep, for it might be the last they would have for many days; and only a few guards kept awake.

There was no danger that the forces of Radzec would strike during the night, and sentinels had been placed along the trails some miles away to give warning of the foe's approach. When that warning was given, the sentinels would run in, and the last ladder be drawn up, and the siege would be on.

Then came the dawn, and the watcher took his place upon the rock and gave the signal, and the sun priest struck the great gong on the roof of the temple. And the people crowded the shelf to face the rising brilliant god and ask that they might come victorious through this war, and that those they loved might be spared.

Some of the headmen gathered on the steps of the temple, thinking that Tanlu would have some last instructions to give them. Word had come from the spies that the army of Radzec would arrive some time during the day, unless it went into camp to await night.

Though they waited for some time, yet Tanlu did not come out and give them speech, and they were about to send a man to ascertain his wishes, when they observed a commotion near the house of the cacique, and heard slaves screaming, and saw women and children running away as if badly frightened.

The headmen forgot Tanlu for the present and hurried along the shelf toward the scene. Before the door of the house slaves were mourning. and they feared that the old cacique had been claimed by death.

But it was a tragedy they faced when they arrived. A slave had gone to the door of the cacique's chamber, bearing the morning food, and half a dozen other slaves were behind him, as was the custom. The skins over the doorway had been drawn back, and the tragedy revealed.

The old cacique was stretched on his bed of furs, his body lifeless, a flint knife sticking in a wound in his throat.

The slaves gave the alarm, and the warriors crowded along the shelf. That their cacique should be struck down at this juncture they considered an ill omen. But it was apparent that his life had been taken foully, and so someone in the pueblo must be such a traitor as to have done the deed.

"Send for the sun priest" the warriors cried.

The priest came, bending forward in grief, for he already had heard the reason for the summons. He looked down upon the body, and made the sun sign on the naked and cold breast, and bade the headmen pick up the corpse and carry it into the temple.

"We must indeed rely upon this Tanlu now!" the priest said. "Let us call him forth and make him acquainted with the sad news!"

But Tanlu was not in his apartment in the temple, and so they sent warriors throughout the pueblo to search for him, and ascertained that he had not gone down the ladder and passed the guards. They searched well, and then reported to the sun priest that Tanlu could not be found.

"He is somewhere about—continue the search for him," the priest said. "And now it is my sorrowful duty to summon the daughter of the sun and tell her the manner of her father's death. Her heart will grieve, for well she loved the old man."

He went to the door of the apartment of the temple maidens, and passed in the word. And word came forth that Dezla was not in the temple. And so the warriors searched throughout the pueblo, for Dezla, the daughter of the sun, as well as for Tanlu.

THE people were chanting their mourning song for the cacique, and in the faces of the warriors was a look that, interpreted, meant they believed the god had turned against them, yet they would fight and die like men. The headmen returned and spoke at length with the sun priest, and then the people were told the truth.

"Here lies the cacique, our master, dead," the sun priest said. "His life was taken by a violent hand. And Tanlu, the man who was named our general, is missing from the pueblo. And Dezla, the daughter of the sun and well-beloved by us, is missing also!"

The people were silent for a moment when they heard the news, and then their anger burst forth.

For there could be but one meaning, they believed. Tanlu, he who had been an outcast of the desert, had played well and with cunning, and had taken revenge for the years he had been forced to live in the open country.

He had slain Prince Lazzano and obtained sanctuary through a trick, thus bringing on a war.

He had caused himself to be made general, and had sent the nobles away with the outcast bands.

And then he had most foully slain the old cacique and had carried away the daughter of the sun, entering the apartments of the maidens of the temple to do so, thereby breaking another law.

Now he had taken the lovely Dezla as a captive, and those of the pueblo were left without a leader and would be at the mercy of Radzec's cruel warriors.

There was instant confusion, then, and the hearts of the warriors were stricken with something like fear, for they had no faith in a victory now and they hoped only to defend themselves as well as they could before the men of Radzec either slew them or captured them and made them slaves.

They scattered along the shelf, each making his own plans for the combat that was coming, two hundred generals where there should have been but one, and all well-arranged plans were forgotten.

The sun priest was in command now that the cacique was dead and had no son or son-in-law to take his place, but the priest was not a warrior and could only talk and urge the men to fight until they died, and the women to handle arrows and carry food and bind up the cuts of the wounded.

Thus the day passed, while black rage against Tanlu grew in every heart in the pueblo. The sun priest climbed the long ladder to the lookout rock once, and stood beside the watcher to look out over the country. He told the watcher the tale, and

Bruxoli said nothing, but looked at the trail and watched for the coming of Radzec's warriors.

The priest went down the ladder again, and still Bruxali stood like a bronze statue and looked over the land below. An hour before sunset the gong on the temple roof was struck, and those on the shelf below saw that the watcher was making signals.

He gave the war signal first and then he swung his arms at his sides, which meant that the enemy was coming, and then extended them toward the west, which meant that the trouble came from that direction.

Then for the first time since he had been named the watcher, Bruxoli left his post at the top of the rock before the evening shadows fell.

He ran to the top of the long ladder, skipped down it and hurried toward the temple. There he bowed thrice before the sun priest.

"What does the watcher wish?" the priest asked.

"I have given the signal, O priest! The enemy is at hand. And I have left my post because the sentinels are running in from the hills and soon the last ladder will be drawn up and we shall stand a siege. There is no need of the watcher on the lookout rock now."

"That is true. You are at liberty to remain below, Bruxoli."

"I have a request, O priest!"

"Say on!"

"Thou hast told me of this man Tanlu, and of how the cacique came to his death, and that the daughter of the sun is gone. Because I am the watcher, I know things of the open country. I ask that I be allowed to leave the pueblo before the last ladder is pulled up, O priest!"

"Thy reason?"

"I will trail this Tanlu to discover whether what we have surmised of this business be truth. I would save the daughter of the sun, if it is the will of the brilliant god."

"Why should the watcher do this thing rather than another man?" the priest asked.

"I am of lowly birth, yet does my heart burn for the daughter of the sun. Since I cannot hope to win her, I must be content with serving her. Bruxoli cannot rest content when her fate is unknown, nor can his arm rest until it has struck down the man who stole her away, or has seen his dead body!"

The priest looked into the watcher's eyes searchingly. and then stretched forth his hands in blessing.

"You are a good man, Bruxoli," he said. "But if you leave the pueblo now, it may be to face death. Radzec's men draw near."

"I can slip away before the ladder is drawn up. It is growing dusk, and Radzec's men will approach slowly and be on guard. I can go toward the east, and make a great circle and so come back west again."

"You do not know which way went Tanlu."

"His people of the open country will know, and they will talk. If Tanlu has done this thing, they will make boast of it, and I will find his trail."

"If he has done this thing? You can doubt it?"

"I looked into Tanlu's eyes and found them good. Hence I doubt it until I find that I am mistaken. If this thing is true, then will my arm have twice its strength because Tanlu forced me to read his character wrongly."

"It is well," the priest said. "You may go. I will send word to the ladder guards."

And so Bruxoli the watcher crept down the ladder the instant before it was drawn up, and drifted into the deep shadows, and so left the pueblo where men were making ready for the battle. Radzec's men, advancing from the west, did not see him.

# CHAPTER IX

THE outcasts moving in five bands each under the lead of a chief, and each band 50 strong, were hidden in a ravine when the army of Radzec passed on the way to the pueblo in the east.

Except for a few sentinels who took stations where they could not be observed the outcasts were hidden beneath an overhanging ledge so that the cacique of the Red Pueblo led his men within a quarter or a league of them without knowing it much to his subsequent sorrow and disgrace.

When the Red Pueblo warriors had disappeared around a hill and it was safe for the outcasts to continue their journey they crept from their places of concealment and made all haste along trails that Radzec did not know existed. It was natural for men bent on war to follow the heights, so as to look down on any foes, but the outcasts followed the watercourses and ravines, and so passed unseen.

They reached the Red Pueblo at night, and it was dark there being no moon because of deep banks or clouds that hung about the horizon. Their chiefs stopped them and sent forward spies, and these spies returned two hours before the dawn with the intelligence that those left behind in the Rea Pueblo feared nothing and did not dream of a hostile band being near at hand.

Through the dense darkness certain ferocious warriors of the open country crept forward. A few old men were guarding the one ladder that remained down, and they died without knowing the identity of those who attacked.

Then the warriors swarmed up the ladder silently, and let down the other ladders, attending promptly to the few men who were awake and on the shelf, and doing it in such a quiet manner that none in the pueblo was aroused.

The false dawn came and the watcher of the Red Pueblo ascended to the lookout rock, prepared to give the signal for the striking of the gong on the temple roof. He looked first far out across the desert in the direction the cacique and his warriors had marched, and then he dropped his eyes and looked below.

He saw the bands of outcasts gathered there at the bottom of the ladders, preparing to greet the rising sun as devout men should, a few of them alert and on guard while the others worshipped.

The man on the lookout rock would have shrieked a warning then, or at least given the signal that meant imminent trouble, but an arrow was shot from below with such good aim that it passed between his shoulder-blades, and he threw his arms out and toppled and fell off the rock and to the ground far below, making not the slightest cry as death claimed him.

The sun peeped above the mountains to the east, and the old man to whom had been assigned the task of striking the temple gong while the warriors were away with their cacique shaded his eyes with his hand and glanced toward the crest of the lookout rock to get the watcher's signal.

He was astonished to find that there was no watcher on the rock, for such a thing was almost beyond belief.

Then to his ears came a chorus of shrill war cries, and he beheld men swarming up the ladders, weapons in their hands and their faces streaked with paint. He struck the gong then with all his might, and repeatedly until its dull boom could be heard above the tumult; yet there was small need for striking it, since those shrill cries had aroused all in the pueblo.

The outcast warriors charged along the lower shelf, scorning to use arrows on such poor prey, and plying their spears. The old men went down before them like grain before a sickle, and the women and children ran to hide in dark corners of the community houses.

A few warriors had been left behind to guard the pueblo, and they gathered now on the steps of the temple, and there made a stand, though they knew that there was no hope of victory and that death would be their lot before much time had passed.

But they fought well, as men will with their backs to a wall, and took their toll of the outcast warriors, which angered the chiefs. And when the last warrior had been sent to join his fathers, these chiefs gave the word to loot.

The cries of the warriors changed now from shouts of warfare to guttural cries of anticipation. They charged into the houses, tearing away the decorated skins hanging before the doors. Fully half of them made their way quickly to the house of the cacique, and began looting there, and carrying their loot out to the shelf to be put in great piles and divided later.

Radzec was a wealthy cacique, and the loot was valuable. They found a niche in the stone where he had hidden his precious gems, and got the riches out. They seized upon decorated skins that told of the prowess of Radzec's ancestors. They carried away a score of jewelled spears, and found others in the houses of the nobles, and put all in the pile on the shelf.

The bodies of the slain were thrown off the rock to the floor of the desert, and the ladders drawn up for fear there might be some living who would escape and carry the news of the assault over the desert to Radzec and that he might give up his siege and return to punish the men of the open country.

And then the searching for women and children began. Here and there they were found crouching in dark corners, and were pulled out. Some of the women shrieked and tried to fight with their bare hands and such inferior weapons as came within their reach, while others merely hung their heads and submitted to their captors with resignation.

The children ran along the lower shelf, and many of them hurled themselves off and were dashed to death on the rocks far below. Those who could be captured were taken, to be carried into the open country and be reared as slaves.

Then came the feast of victory. One man was sent to the crest of the lookout rock to watch for foes, and the others made merry around the fires. They looted the houses for food and drink, and what they could not consume or carry away they destroyed.

They slew every goat, every domestic animal. And they sang their war cries as they danced around the captives, while the women crouched in fear against the front of the temple, and huddled their children to their breasts.

Then the chieftains got together and walked slowly up the steps to the temple door, some of the nobles following at their heels. Outcast nobles and chieftains they had been, but now they were conquerors.

They went through the wide door and so stood in the main room of the temple, and an under-priest came down from the altar and confronted them, for the high priest of the sun had gone with Radzec to ask the brilliant god for victory to his arms, and mayhap to seize upon some precious bit of loot for himself.

"What do you here?" the under-priest asked.

"We come as conquerors," one of the headmen replied.

"You are outcasts of the desert?"

"We were such; now we are conquerors."

"This is a temple of the brilliant god."

"And this be war, hence there is no sanctuary until it is at an end."

"You may not defile the temple."

"That is true! But because we are conquerors we can claim anything that is within its walls, O priest!"

"What would you?" the priest asked.

"The jewels that are in thy keeping!"

"It is the law that conquerors may take any precious jewels that are not in the altar of the brilliant god. Who am 1 to stand against conquerors? The jewels are in that small room there!" The priest pointed to a doorway covered with painted skins, and two of the nobles went to get the jewels.

"WHAT would you now?" the priest asked, since the chieftains did not go away.

"There are other jewels."

"In the altar of the brilliant god—yes! Would you touch them? Would you defy the god himself?"

"Not so," one of the chieftains replied. "The god is beloved by us. Yet there are other precious jewels that we claim."

"I know not your meaning."

"You do not choose to know it, you mean. These other jewels I mention are your temple maidens."

"No, no!" the priest cried. "Would you touch the fairest maidens in the land?"

"That we would! As conquerors we are entitled to seize them. Where have you hidden them?"

"They are not hidden. They crouch in their apartment, in deadly fear. Yet you shall not have them."

"What will prevent?"

The priest walked briskly some feet to one side, and took up his stand before a doorway.

"I will prevent, to the best of my poor ability," he said.

"You take upon yourself the duties of a warrior, priest!" one of the chieftains cried. "Stand aside, else we are privileged to forget thy priesthood."

"I shall not stand aside. Look upon me not as priest, but as man!" he cried.

The chieftain who had spoken raised a hand, and half a dozen of the nobles rushed forward. And so the under-priest died and dropped to the floor of the temple.

It was dark in the apartment, but there were torches fastened to the walls, and one of these was illuminated from the fire nearest the temple.

The chieftains ran rapidly through the rooms, kicking at the piles of furs and skins, and finally they came to the last room of all. And there they found the score of temple maidens, each selected for her good birth and beauty.

They were dressed simply in some white clinging stuff, their luxuriant hair caught up with fillets or golden bands studded with precious stones. The chieftains stopped in surprise, for never had there been seen before such an array of beauty—even among temple maidens.

"Which is the daughter of the sun?" the spokesman asked.

One of them stepped forward a pace, a glorious maiden of 16 years, who stood erect and proud before them.

"I am the daughter of the sun!" she said. "I am the granddaughter of Radzec!"

"You are prizes of war," the chieftain said. "You—and all these maidens."

"I have kept faith, O cacique!" Sazzac told Radzec. "Here is Dezla, daughter of the sun."

"And what manner of men are you?" she asked. "You are not from the pueblo to the east, where my grandfather has gone to make war."

"We are of the open country!"

"Outcasts?" she sneered. "You wait until our warriors have gone away on a campaign, and then come like cowards to work your will?"

"Not so. We are allied with the pueblo to the east. Tanlu is our great chieftain. We make war according to the law."

"Then we may expect no mercy," the daughter of the sun said.

"This thing has come upon you because your grandfather sought to wed his unworthy son to that other fair daughter of the sun who lives in the pueblo to the east," she was told. "It is war, and all within the law."

"What would you do with us?" she asked.

"Take you to our huts in the desert, O maiden of the temple. You shall be my wife. It will be an honorable post."

"The woman of an outcast!"

"Stigma will be removed from our name for this warfare, and we will perhaps come to this Red Pueblo to live. And these other maidens, because of their high birth and beauty, will not be slaves, but will be the women of other chieftains and nobles."

"Death were better than such a fate!" she cried.

"It is war!" he replied, and signed to the men behind him to take the maidens.

The daughter of the sun gave a cry and brought her hands before her. Before one could utter a warning a flint knife had flashed, and the spokesman reeled backward and fell, wounded to the death. And then the daughter of the sun turned the knife upon herself, and drove it into her breast, and so died.

Behind her, the other maidens of the temple brought forth knives, and, crying their supplications to the brilliant god, they drove them into their breasts, before a man could spring forward to hinder. And so the score of maidens of the temple came to their earthly end.

The chieftains stalked from the temple and went down the long flight of steps, and then there was more feasting; and presently one of the guards gave an alarm, and they beheld a lone man riding toward the pueblo on a pony urging his mount to a breakneck pace.

" 'Tis Tanlu," cried one. " 'Tis Tanlu, our leader! Has there been a disaster in the east?"

They crowded around the tops of the ladders, and one of the headmen went down to meet Tanlu. He sprang from his pony and hurried to the chieftain.

"There has been success?" he asked.

"Everything has been successful, Tanlu. There is a a huge amount of loot."

"You have done well, then."

"The women and children haver been made captives and shut in one of the community houses. But
the maidens of the temple slew themselves, oh,
Tanlu, when we tried to seize them!"

"They were fools. Perhaps I might have spared
them as an offering to the brilliant god because of
our victory."

"How are things in the east?"

"I know not. Last night I slipped away, and came
here to see how it went with you. I was afraid some
of the outcast bands might get out of hand and become scattered, and it is necessary to keep all together for the remainder of the campaign. I feared
that they might go back to their huts with the loot."

"Radzec besieges the pueblo to the east?"

"I presume so. They did not need me there for
the time being. With their backs to the wall, the men
of the eastern pueblo will fight for days, and before
Radzec and his warriors find a way to their shelf we
will be at their rear, and none shall escape."

Tanlu made up the long ladder then, and those
on the shelf shrieked a welcome at him. He stood on
the steps of the temple and ordered that the loot be
piled before him.

"There is to be an equal division," he said, "but it
will not be made until the war is at an end. You men
are yet to fight the forces of Radzec, and among
those surviving this loot will be distributed. Hence it

is to the advantage of every man that he guard his life well and battle to such purpose that he live while his enemies die."

Then Tanlu raised a hand in salute when they cheered him, and went down the steps and to one of the fires, where he demanded food and drink, for he was fatigued because of his journey. Not only had he ridden from the pueblo to the east. but also he had gone aside into the open country to give certain commands to the men remaining there in case of a disaster to his men. Tanlu was a chieftain who provided against every emergency.

The Red Pueblo was put to rights then, and the dead temple maidens and the priest who had defended them were tossed from the rock to the desert floor. Guards were selected carefully and sent to their posts, and sentinels went out to the hills.

The children lost a part of their fear and played about the shelf, and some of the men from the open country picked them up and tossed them about, telling them what a great time they would have in the desert.

"It has come to my mind," said Tanlu, "that a thing to please all may come to pass if the forces of Radzec are wiped out. In that case there will be here a goodly pueblo without inhabitants. We men of the desert will enter and take possession, and so live proper lives. See to it, then, that the forces of Radzec are slain!"

They greeted the announcement with cheers, for this was a thing near their hearts, since they were tired of living as outcasts. And then they began sharpening their spears again, getting ready to wipe Radzec and his warriors from the face of the earth.

The long day passed, and Tanlu selected the men who were to remain at the Red Pueblo and guard the loot and the women, and then prepared for his rest, so that he might be strong and refreshed at dawn when the army marched.

He stretched himself upon a bed of skins in Radzec's house and thought of the events of the day,. and of what a great man he had become, and would become a greater one yet. He thought of Dezla, daughter of the sun, and was well pleased.

And a man came out of the desert and was halted by the guards at the bottom of the ladder.

"I am the watcher at the pueblo to the east!" he said. "Bruxoli is my name! I seek Tanlu!"

"Tanlu is in the pueblo. There has been disaster in the east? You bring bad news?"

"Such news as I have is not told to every man who asks!" the watcher retorted. "Take me to Tanlu!"

"You may pass up the ladder!"

Bruxoli went up, and found a chiefthin and told his name and purpose, and was ushered to the cacique's house. And Tanlu, just falling asleep, heard his name called and sat up on his bed of skins. He saw Bruxoli, the watcher, standing before him like a statue, his arms folded across his breast.

"I have come, Tanlu!" he said.

## CHAPTER X

RADZEC'S army surrounded the pueblo to the east with surprising speed, driving in the sentinels without capturing a single one, however, and at once building great fires in a circle around the place, and established a line of warriors in such manner that none could escape and flee to the open country.

Then the warriors of the Red Pueblo danced around their fires and sang their war songs, which told of what they intended to do in the way of slaughter when the dawn came and the battle began.

Up on the shelf of the pueblo the men worked hard, yet without spirit, for since the cacique was dead and Tanlu gone, and the daughter of the sun not there to urge them to greater bravery, they had little hope of standing off Radzec's bold warriors for any length of time.

They got the piles of rocks ready to hurl down upon the heads of Radzec's men, and saw that arrows were handy and bows well strung; and the women heated water to throw into the faces of their foes, though water might prove a precious thing later, if the siege was a long one.

Rocks were heated, too, to be used as weapons, and food was placed where the warriors could get it when it was needed without leaving the edge of the shelf.

From pure defiance, the warriors of the eastern pueblo chanted their war songs, too, and the women aided them, and the children were sent to places of safety far inside the community houses. And then the dawn came, and the man who had been assigned to take Bruxoli's place stood on the rock and gave the signal despite the cloud of arrows that flew about him, and escaped unscathed, which many took to be an omen.

The gong on the roof of the temple struck, and every man and woman in the pueblo knelt and faced the rising sun, and asked the brilliant god to be their friend in this battle, and to punish with everlasting misery all traitors and men who showed themselves to be craven in their hearts.

And then the battle began!

This was not like the small fight at the Red Pueblo that same day. Here there was opposition of a sort, and the pueblo was on guard and prepared.

The sun priest painted out the marks on his fore-head and assumed command, since he was the only man present who had the right, and did the best he could to make himself over into a warrior. But his orders were disregarded for the most part by the warriors, for they recognized that he knew little of the art of warfare, and each man fought the battle in his own way.

Clouds of arrows struck against the sides of the pueblo, and many of the defenders were wounded and the women made haste to attend them, that they might take their places in the ranks again. Radzec's men tried to throw ladders against the rock, but they were hurled back, and the warriors of the Red Pueblo with them.

The defenders shot arrows in reply, and Radzec's forces suffered heavily, being in the open, but that was to be expected in such warfare. Stones were hurled down upon them, and hot water thrown in their faces, but they did not retreat even as much as to get breath for a fresh assault.

Throughout the day they battled, and then came the night, and Radzec's warriors built the big fires again, so that all sides of the pueblo were light. The defenders had to watch carefully during the night, too, for once before Radzec had won a pueblo by putting ladders against the walls while the defenders were off guard.

And then cane the second dawn of the struggle,

and the battle raged again. Radzec's men were infuriated now because so many of their comrades had been slain, and they showed double the bravery they had the day before, so that the defenders found themselves compelled to waste twice as much ammunition.

Radzec's men took to shooting balls of fire on their arrows, something that was then new to war, and repeatedly they drove the men back from the edge of the ledge, but always the defenders returned before the ladders could be put in place and men swarm up them.

The sun was at its height when the priest received an arrow through his breast and died. Now the warriors had none at all to lead them, for they would not listen to those who attempted to take the post of commander for the time being. They fought on, and meanwhile quarrelled among themselves.

Twice Radzec's warriors won to the lower ledge, but were beaten off again, and each time the beating cost the lives of many of the defenders. Radzec could afford to lose men, having so many, but the defenders could not.

Those of the pueblo knew that another day would see them defeated, either slain or made into slaves, their goods taken, their women seized, and their children reared to be turned into beasts of burden.

And so it began to be whispered about that perhaps it would be wiser to make arrangements with Radzec, that they might be spared. It were better to be a slave than to be a dead man, said some, though, others thought not and promised to die on their own spears before surrendering.

But the counsel of those who wished to surrender prevailed, and the others agreed to listen to Radzec's terms at least, and decide after they had heard them. And so the fighting ceased suddenly, and one of the headmen went to the edge of the shelf and spread wide his hands, the palms down, in a sign that he wished to parley.

Radzec's men ceased their battling, and after a time the cacique himself stepped forward and stood beneath the shelf, some of his nobles behind him.

"What is it you wish, dogs of the eastern pueblo?" he demanded.

"I have been appointed to hold speech with thee, Radzec," the spokesman said, "and when I talk it is as if with the words of all here."

"Say on!"

"We would make arrangements with thee that this bloodshed might come to an end."

"Where is thy cacique? Let him come forward and make the talk. Radzec does not hold converse with underlings."

"Our cacique is dead, O Radzec! Two dawns ago we found him on his bed of skins with a knife in his throat."

"He deserved the death! Say on!"

"It is believed that Tanlu the outcast slew him, for when we found him dead we found also that this Tanlu was gone, and so was the daughter of the sun, and we think this Tanlu forced her to go with him. So we have none of rank to lead us, O Radzec, and we cannot fight your warriors well.

"If you grant us terms, then will we lay down our arms and cease battling; if you do not, then will we die to the last man and slay our women and children and destroy all our goods—and so you will gain nothing, and your men shall have given their lives for naught."

Radzec took thought of that, walking back and forth below the shelf, his hand caressing his chin. If the old cacique was dead and these men without a leader, he saw possibilities. A pueblo denuded of goods and men would do him no good, since he would have to people it with inhabitants of his own.

But if he could make peace, these men and women could be ruled by him, and another strong pueblo be built up under his rule, and he could send some noble of his to be cacique, and thus enlarge his empire.

"What terms do you wish?" he asked presently.

"What has the great Radzec to offer?"

"You will pay for your lives 1,000 goats, to be delivered as speedily as possible at the Red Pueblo. You will surrender the precious stones your cacique had in his house, and all others in the pueblo, and any decorated skins belonging to your nobles that I see fit to take. Fifty male children you must give up to be reared as slaves of the Red Pueblo, and we shall select them from the group.

"A like number of women will be selected by us, preferably those of noble blood and maidens of your temple, and these shall be given to my warriors to be either wives or slaves. And you will lay down all weapons. and be guarded by my men until these things are done."

"Say on!" the spokesman chanted in a hollow voice.

"Being assured that you have no longer thoughts of war, I shall allow you full liberty, and you shall live as before, except that none of you shall have rank. My nobles will be sent to be your headmen, and I shall send one from the Red Pueblo to be your cacique. My terms have been spoken; I am done!"

The spokesman turned to confer with those near him on the shelf. After a time he called down to Radzec again.

"Having no chieftain to decide for us, we must argue this thing and find the will of the majority," he said.

"The brilliant god now is sinking to his rest. We ask that until the dawn there be no more fighting; and we shall spend the night coming to a decision. At dawn will we let thee know whether the terms are accepted."

"It is well," Radzec said; for he knew the short hours of peace could not aid the defenders much if they decided to reject the terms at dawn, and during those same hours his warriors could strengthen their positions and gain rest, and the dead could be buried and those wounded receive attention.

Radzec threw wide his arms in a gesture that the conference was at an end, and passed the word that fighting was to be stopped until the dawn, yet at the same time he bade his men be on guard against any possible treachery. Up on the shelf the defenders watched for treachery, too, having as little faith in Radzec as he had in them.

The night fires were built, and the defenders ate a meal, and then there was a conference in the temple. Because there was no leader and every man wanted to say his thoughts, the conference was a thing of hours.

The temple maidens chanted their sorrow in their apartment, for well they knew their fate if the surrender became a fact. They would be taken by the victors, because they were of good birth and beautiful, and while they could not be made slaves, yet each felt that it was beneath her to become the wife of one of Radzec's warriors. For wives taken in battle were seldom respected, having come without courting, and often were set aside later when the warrior decided to wed with one of his own tribe.

The women of the pueblo wailed, too, each be-
lieving that if the surrender was made she would be
one selected to be a slave, and would be torn from
husband and children, or if a maid from sweetheart,
and possibly never see them again. And each mother
who had men children clasped them to breast, fear-
ing her child would be one selected, and would be
reared to be a beast of burden and forced to feed
with the dogs and goats and know the sorrow that
can be held in the breast of a slave.

Many there were who urged that the pueblo fight
to the last, and then every woman and child be slain
just before Radzec was victorious, so that none
would fall into his hands. The temple maidens decided to slay themselves, as the ones in the Red
Pueblo had done though they did not know of this.

But there were men in the assembly to whom life
was dear, and they were willing to give up goats and
jewels and women and children; and in the end their
counsel prevailed. They put the matter to a vote, all
agreeing to abide by the decision of the majority.

Any warrior who did not wish to surrender might
slay himself with honor, it was agreed, but the temple maidens and women were to be guarded so that
they could do themselves no harm.

They voted, and the decision of the majority was
for the surrender to Radzec at dawn. Then the
women wailed the more, and the children tried to
hide themselves, and the warriors paced back and

forth along the ledges with their heads hung on their breasts, refusing to meet one another's eyes, their pride crushed. Many had determined to fall upon their own spears when the dawn came.

Finally the long night was at an end, the night all wished might last forever, and the first red streak of the dawn appeared over the mountains to the east. The gong on the temple roof was struck, and the people of the pueblo knelt where they happened to be and faced the brilliant god, praying that in some miraculous fashion all would yet be well.

Radzec came from the hut that his men had erected for him, and stood beneath the ledge. The spokesman went out and looked down at the cacique.

"Thy answer?" Radzec asked.

The spokesman threw up his head and looked at the brilliant god and said a prayer for his people, and then he spread his palms in the peace sign and looked down at Radzec again.

"We have decided to agree to thy terms, O cacique" he cried. "And we ask thee to remember the brilliant god and his goodness, and in his name be merciful!"

## CHAPTER XI

TANLU rubbed his sleepy eyes and looked up at Bruxoli in astonishment as the watcher stood straight and proud before him, his arms folded across his chest. Then he sprang to his feet and walked a couple of steps forward.

"What is it?" he asked.

"Will the great Tanlu send these slaves away that I may speak with him privately?"

"They are not slaves, but my comrades, yet will I send them away," Tanlu said.

He indicated that he wished to be alone with the newcomer, and the guards withdrew. And then Tanlu motioned for Bruxoli to sit on the skin bed, and was somewhat surprised when the watcher refused.

"There is somethin in thy appearance, Bruxoli, that promises dire news," Tanlu said. "It is not possible that things have gone amiss at the pueblo to the east."

"Why are you here, Tanlu?" Bruxoli asked.

"Is that not a bold question for a man to ask of his general?"

"In ordinary times it were, Tanlu; but this is not an ordinary occasion. I have trailed you from the pueblo, and find thee here."

"Why have you trailed me, O watcher?"

"You do well to call me watcher, for not only have I watched from the summit of the lookout rock, but also have I striven to watch over the welfare of those dear to me."

"Let us come down to the business of this visit," Tanlu said. "How is it that you are not in the pueblo aiding in defending it against its foes?"

"And why are you, the general and leader, not there?" Bruxoli asked in return.

"I like not the manner of your speech, but since I know you for a loyal and peculiar man, I will make reply. Those in the pueblo are safe, for they can defend it against Radzec's men for days. But I was anxious regarding these bands of outcasts, afraid that they would obtain much loot and neglect to return and attack Radzec in the rear. So I slipped away to meet with them and direct them back instantly, knowing that those in the pueblo could make a defence until I returned with these warriors."

"Why did not you say this to the men in the

pueblo, instead of creeping away in the night?"

"Because the idea came to me after the most of them were asleep. Besides, some might have objected to my going, though I knew it was for the best. And in desperation they will fight Radzec the harder when a leader is missing, and my reappearance with the outcasts will rally them."

"Where is Dezla, the beautiful daughter of the sun?"

"Safe in the temple, I presume, praying to the brilliant god for her people's success, and praying also, I hope, for me."

"You say this to me?"

"Why not?" Tanlu asked. "What means this mysterious manner of thine, Bruxoli?"

Now they stood only a pace apart, and looked deep into each other's eyes, for they were standing just under a torch and could see plainly. Presently the watcher sighed.

"Thank the brilliant god that thou art an honest man!" he said.

"What mean you? Had you doubt of me? Did those of the pueblo think I had forsaken them?"

"They did," Bruxoli replied. "All that—and more!"

"What mean you? Say on!"

"When the dawn came, it was found that you were gone. At first it was believed you were somewhere about the pueblo, and guards were sent to find you, for the headmen wished a council of war.

At the same time the slaves of the old cacique took him his morning food."

"Well?"

"They found the old cacique dead, Tanlu—slain—a knife sticking in his throat. He had been slain most foully during the night."

"Who did such a thing?"

"The people soon said that Tanlu had done it."

"Now by the august and brilliant god—"

"Make no oath yet, Tanlu, my friend. For I may call you friend now, being convinced that the suspicions were unworthy. Hear the remainder of my tale. The cacique was slain, and you were gone, and Dezla, the daughter of the sun, was gone also."

"The daughter of the sun?"

"Even so. She was not in the temple—she was not in all the pueblo. And so men said that, for some fancied wrong, you had turned traitor and slain the cacique, and then had carried Dezia away. Moreover, that left them without a leader for this war. They said, too, that it was a trick that you sent the nobles away with the outcasts—that it was merely to leave them without a man to whom they could look for authority. And they hinted that perhaps it was all a trick, and that you were one of Radzec's men!"

Tanlu looked his astonishment for an instant, and then gave a cry of rage. He grasped Bruxoli by the arm.

"They believed that?" he cried. "They thought me

such a man? By the brilliant god, they deserve to be vanquished."

"'Think, Tanlu! How did it look?"

"True! It did look as if I were guilty."

"And I, who knew you and believed your heart was good, even thought it was so."

"Bruxoli!"

"I am sorry for it now. I went to the sun priest and obtained permission to take your trail. I meant to search until I found you. and if you had done these things, to kill you!"

"Were I guilty, that would be just."

"But I did not find Dezla here."

"And where is she?" Tanlu cried. "Where is the daughter of the sun? Who has carried her away?"

"Those are questions I cannot answer, Tanlu."

"And what are the people of the pueblo doing without a leader—without even the old cacique to urge them to battle?"

"They must be in sore straits, Tanlu."

"Wait! I have a thought!" Tanlu said.

He paced the floor, and stopped near a corner to look through an aperture at the fires burning below. He remembered when last he had spoken to the daughter of the sun. "Beware of Sazzac!" she had told him.

Sazzac!

THE thought struck Tanlu with the force of a

blow—Sazzac was the man! Sazzac had escaped from the outcast band and had returned to the pueblo at night. He could pass the guards easily, being a noble chieftain, and even command their silence as to his visit. Sazzac had slain the old cacique, and had carried away the daughter of the sun! Sazzac hoped by some trick, perhaps, to gain the mastery over the pueblo, to wed Dezla, and make himself cacique.

"Come, Bruxoli, with me!" Tanlu cried.

All thought of rest had left Tanlu now. He raced along the shelf with the watcher at his heels, and ran down the ladder, and hurried to where the headmen of the outcasts had their fire. He called the chief headman to him.

"With which band is Sazzac, the man who attempted treason?" Tanlu asked.

"With the band of sentinels, oh, Tanlu!"

"And where may they be found?"

"The men are scattered over the hills watching the trails. But their temporary home camp is at the head of the ravine, where you can see the reflection of the fires."

Tanlu started running again, and Bruxoli kept close behind him. They reached the ravine, panting and almost exhausted, and Tanlu called the headman before him.

"Where is Sazzac, the treasonable noble given into thy keeping?" Tanlu asked.

The headman dropped to his knees and held up his hands.

"Mercy, oh, Tanlu!" he cried. "Soon after we had left the pueblo to the east this Sazzac slipped away from us. I think he hid himself under the ledge when Radzec's men were passing us, and remained there when we marched on."

"Why was it not reported to me at once?" Tanlu demanded.

"I feared to report it, O Tanlu! Besides, what trouble could come of it? The man is alone in the desert. which he knows not. Either hunger and thirst will claim him, else he will fall into the hands of Radzec's warriors and be slain."

"A great trouble has come of it," Tanlu said in a terrible voice. "The man returned to the pueblo. He slew the old cacique, and he carried away Dezla, the daughter of the sun. No doubt he would have slit my throat also, but I already had left the pueblo. And so those at the pueblo are fighting without a leader, and the fairest maid in the land is in the hands of a scoundrel."

"Mercy, Tanlu!" the headman cried.

"This much and no more—that I give you permission to fall upon your own spear!"

"Tanlu—"

"I have spoken!"

Tanlu folded his arms and stood back. The headman extended his hands toward his leader, but there was no response. He glanced at the other men about him, and they turned their faces away.

And so he picked up his spear and stepped a little way aside, and once more he looked back at Tanlu; and then he braced the spear against a rock on the ground, and put the point of it against his breast just over his heart.

"It is just!" he said in a hoarse voice.

The next instant they saw the head of the spear plunge through his back, and his lifeless body toppled to one side.

"Give him proper burial!" Tanlu directed the dead headman's followers. "He disobeyed orders, and hence was a poor warrior and not fit to live; but also he paid the penalty without faltering and hence was a brave warrior and deserves to be remembered as such!"

Then Tanlu turned and rushed back to the pueblo, and the watcher ran at his heels. Tanlu caused the alarm to be sounded, and the men were roused from sleep to receive their orders.

"Make all haste, all except the men who were named to remain here as guards!" Tanlu directed. "Return swiftly to the pueblo to the east and attack the warriors of Radzec from behind! There shall be loot and women and slaves for those who fight well and escape death!

"But make haste, for those at the pueblo to the east are in sore straits! Let not a single man of

Radzec's escape your spears and arrows! And watch the open country, and pick up every man there and hold him for me. And take this Radzec alive if you can, and hold him also for me!"

The words were passed, and the warriors cheered and prepared for their departure. Tanlu stood on the edge of the ledge, his arms folded across his breast again, and looked down upon them. Those who had ponies sprang to their backs and scampered ahead, to watch the country and prevent surprise. The others gathered up weapons and food, and vessels filled with water, and crowded forward about their headmen.

"March!" Tanlu commanded, waving his arms at them.

They brandished their spears and shrieked at him, and began the march. Swinging their bodies from side to side they strode rapidly past the line of fires and into the dense darkness ahead their few torches gleaming in the distance like fireflies.

Soon all except the last band were gone, and its headman came up to Tanlu.

"You will have us for escort?" he asked.

"I do not march with you!"

"You remain here?" asked the headman.

"Do you question my comings and goings?" Tanlu demanded, whirling upon him.

"Your pardon, Tanlu!"

"You have it—but get you gone! Your men are

waiting! Did I not say to make all haste? Our brothers at the pueblo to the east may be dying for want of aid."

The headman bowed thrice and hurried away, glad that his breath remained in his body.

Tanlu watched until the torches no longer could be seen in the distance; and then he whirled around and faced the watcher.

"You came on a pony?" he asked.

"Yes, Tanlu."

"Did you follow a trail, or did you ask for Tanlu?"

"I was a fool. I merely asked for Tanlu, and found that you had passed toward the Red Pueblo, and traced you here."

"You were a fool, indeed. Had you followed the trail, you might have found the daughter of the sun and the renegade Sazzac before this, and rescued the maiden or else died in the attempt. Your pony is a good one?"

"There are not many swifter, Tanlu."

"Do you wish to go with me?"

"Where are you going?"

"To mount my own pony and ride like the wind toward the open country. By dawn I would be near the pueblo to the east, ahead of these, my troops. And there I shall take up the trail of the man who carried away the daughter of the sun, and I shall come up with him if he be still alive.

"And I shall not rest nor think of other things until that man is dead and the daughter of the sun is clasped in mine arms. For I love her, Bruxoli, and will save her or die! I fear not for the other pueblo; the outcasts will drive Radzec's men away or slay them. What say you, Bruxoli?"

"I will ride by your side, O Tanlu! And your oaths shall be my oaths!"

"It is well! Come!"

## CHAPTER XII

RADZEC, hearing from the spokesman that the pueblo had decided to accept his terms, turned to the nobles behind him and spoke in whispered tones.

"The weaklings have agreed, noble warriors. What say you now?"

"The plan of which we spoke during the night is the best, O cacique," one replied.

"I had thought, before you mentioned the plan, that it would be an excellent thing to let these men live, and thus we would have a pueblo already peopled, and would have but to put a cacique and nobles over them."

"Yet our words hold good, cacique! A people governed against its will is never governed properly. After a few days there will be conspiracies and trouble will follow. They will worry out our lives with con-

tinual watching. There will be little outbreaks, and
perhaps the cacique you name will have his throat
slit some night, and the nobles be slaughtered one at
a time. Punishment would follow, of course, yet that
would not bring back to life the cacique and the nobles."

"That is true. What would you then?" Radzec
asked.

"What we proposed, O cacique. Bid them let
down all the ladders and stand back on the steps of
the temple. Then we will ascend with our warriors,
and have these men place their arms in a great pile.
We will order them to bring the women and children before us, so that we may pick fifty of each,
and you will have them name certain ones to see
that the prize goats are gathered from the hills and
driven to the Red Pueblo."

"And then—?"

"Then, when they think all is well and are going
about their task, do you give a signal, O cacique, and
our warriors will fall upon the unarmed men, and
slay them all, and throw their bodies off the rock.
Then we may take all the women that please us, re-
moving some to the Red Pueblo to be slaves and
forcing the others to remain here. We can do the
same with the children."

"What follows?"

"The Red Pueblo. as you know. has too many inhabitants, and we must build more houses, and

enlarge those we have, which will be a difficult task, else turn some of our people out into the open country. Why not send a part of our people here to populate this pueblo, which is ready for occupancy?

"Send likewise a priest, and a man to be cacique, and some nobles to help him rule. Then will you know, oh, Radzec, that all men in this pueblo are loyal, and thou shalt be lord over two strong pueblos. From here, also, you can make war on those of the south who have been the allies of these people."

"That is an excellent thought and worthy of a great noble!" Radzec claimed. "And it will be rare sport for my warriors to work their will on unarmed men."

"Also it will keep them in an excellent humor, oh, cacique, and make them praise thy name."

"Let it be done as has been said, then." Radzac ordered. "I wish to please my subjects."

He looked up at the spokesman again and threw out his arms in a gesture that he had orders to give.

"You will let fall all the ladders immediately," he ordered. "All your warriors will put their weapons in a great pile on the ledge, and then gather on the steps of the temple. My men will ascend, and then you will name some of your people to gather the prize goats and collect the jewels, and bring forth your women and children that we may select our 50 of each."

The spokesman bowed and left the edge of the

shelf, and Radzec turned again to his chieftains and ordered them to assemble their men where the ends of the ladders would fall, and also explain the proposed strategy to them.

But there was a whispered consultation up on the shelf and so far back from its edge that those below could not see. A man who had been walking on the roof of the temple had looked toward the west, and had seen a sight that had astonished him. For men were coming from the west, great numbers of men in great haste.

Those of the pueblo did not know whether they were the outcasts returning, or whether they were more of Radzec's men who had beaten the outcasts and now had come to join their cacique.

"Let us lake our time, until we know what is to come," one of them proposed. "It were folly to let down the ladders if these men coming over the hills are our friends. And I fear treachery if the ladders are let down."

"So do I," another replied.

And then a headman remembered that it had been part of Tanlu's plan that the outcasts should destroy the Red Pueblo and then return and attack Radzec in the rear.

A man stood out boldly on the temple roof and signalled to the approaching men, and one of Radzec's chieftains saw him. And immediately thereafter Radzec and his warriors observed the menace.

There was small question then as to whether those coming from the west were friends or foes. Battle cries sounded from the warriors of Radzec, and they grasped their weapons and charged forward to meet this new foe.

But the outcasts remembered the cruelties of years, and they hated Radzec and the people of the Red Pueblo. They met the charge with great courage and soon the plain before the pueblo was the scene of a great battle in which every man sought him an individual foe and had a private battle of his own.

Radzec's men were beaten back to the walls of the pueblo, and now those within, having hope born anew, entered the fight again. They sent volleys of arrows down upon their enemies and hurled their rocks, and Radzec found himself caught between two forces each of which was trying to destroy him.

He called to his chieftains, and they rallied their men and began fighting away from the pueblo and to a certain small hill not far distant. Repeatedly the outcasts charged, urged on by their headmen, and remembering what Tanlu had told them considering a division of the loot of the Red Pueblo, they fought with twice their usual bravery.

Radzec began to feel some fear for these ferocious men of the open country did not seem to know the meaning of cowardice, and it appeared that all had made their peace with the brilliant god, since they were so ready to die. But he urged on his warriors and gained some slight advantage for an instant, and so fought back his foes.

And then the ladders were dropped at the pueblo behind them, and the warriors poured down them and went into the fight hand-to-hand, and the old men remaining on the ledge pulled the ladders up again, so Radzec's men could not enter if they were victorious.

The cacique of the Red Pueblo found himself between two forces indeed now, and managed to swerve aside with his men, thus bringing the outcasts and the men of the pueblo together and having all his foes in front. It was a clever move, and showed his generalship.

He was striving to make for the hill now, for it was so arranged that it could be approached easily from only one side, and it was an excellent place for a force of men to stand at bay. Radzec wanted to get his warriors there, where the foe could be held off for a time and his men gather breath and courage. He imagined, too that the frenzy of the foe would die down if they were stopped for a time; Radzec knew many things concerning the workings of men's minds.

He communicated the plans to his chieftains, and his forces fell back step by step, fighting continually the men dropping here and there in numbers that brought anguish to Radzec's heart. And finally he gained the hill and his men swarmed up after him, And there the outcasts and the men of the pueblo were held in check.

Radzec protected his flanks and rear, and then called his chieftains to him for conference.

"These foes are outcasts of the desert," he said. "I presume that this Tanlu, who slew my son, has gathered them, and perhaps does lead them. Shall the proud warriors of the Red Pueblo be beaten by such folk?"

But the outcasts did not give before the charge, and many of Radzec's men fell, and the remainder retreated up the slope, running from the clouds of arrows that pursued them.

The brilliant god went from sight and the dusk came, and Radzec realized that nothing more could be accomplished that day. So he put out heavy guards and bade his men rest on their arms. Small fires were built with dry sticks and grass, and meat was eaten.

And down at the bottom of the slope the outcasts and the warriors of the pueblo built then fires and ate their meat, too, and were content to wait.

## CHAPTER XIII

DEZLA, the daughter of the sun, was of slight build; also she had been reared in luxury and never had worked with her muscles at stern tasks. Hence great strength was not hers and she was like a helpless babe in the clutch of Sazzac. He had found her while she slept in the temple, had stifled the cries of alarm she would have voiced and had carried her down one of the ladders and to his waiting pony. He had thrown her across the mount before him, and slipped away from the pueblo.

They travelled until it was almost dawn, and then Sazzac stopped at the head of a ravine where there was a tiny stream of water.

Now Dezla saw his face for the first time and realized who had abducted her, and was greatly astonished,

"What is the meaning of this violence, Sazzac?"

she demanded. "You are bold to treat the daughter of the cacique in such manner."

" 'Tis a time of war, fair Dezla, and a chieftain is entitled to use his own strategies," he made answer.

"Has the noble Sazzac turned renegade?"

"No harm will come to the fair daughter of the sun," he said. "I have but saved her, and she shall have every honor due her rank, if she will obey. Evil days have fallen upon our people. The cacique, your father, had grown weak in his old age. Myself, with some of the other nobles, did try to save him. But he named an outcast to be our general, and the nobles would not serve under such a man."

"I heard of that. And you tried to play treason, and this Tanlu prevented you," she cried.

"You heard correctly, O Dezla. And this Tanlu scattered the nobles among the outcast tribes, so that he could work his will in our absence."

"What mean you?"

"That he is in reality a man of the Red Pueblo. He serves Radzec. He was playing to weaken us, so that we would fall easy victims to this Radzec, and he has succeeded. But I escaped from the outcast chief who had me in charge and under cover of night returned to the pueblo. And there I found that this Tanlu had slipped away, and before he went he did a disgraceful thing. For the cacique, your father, was murdered on his bed. I found him so when I crept into his house to tell him my purpose."

"My father dead?" she cried.

She would have wept, then, but her pride forbade her.

"Say on—Sazzac," she whispered.

"I crept around and learned several things. There is small hope that those of the pueblo can stand against Radzec's warriors, and so I decided to save you, O Dezla."

"Could you not have awakened me and told me so? Was it necessary to use violence to carry me from the temple?"

"I feared you would want to go to your father, and that the alarm would be given, and that then we would have no chance to leave the pueblo."

"And now?" she asked.

"Now I am free, and I have saved you. We will remain here in the open country until we see how things are going. When it is over we shall return to the pueblo, and I shall be cacique, and you shall be my wife. If you have vengeance to call down, call it down upon this outcast Tanlu!"

"Sazzac, he is a better man than you!" she cried. "He is more loyal and braver and in every way a more noble man. And his blood is as good as yours! What you have been telling me is a mass of lies! You slew my father with your own cowardly hand!"

The dawn had come now, and she saw his face livid with fury when she looked up at him.

"Have it as you please, Dezla of the sun!" he

sneered. "However, I shall be cacique when this sorry business is over, and you shall be my wife."

"Never will Dezla of the sun marry you!" she cried vehemently. "Rather would I stand before the priest with a goatherd!"

"So this outcast Tanlu hath claimed thy heart?" he asked.

"I have not said so. But I do say that he is thrice the man you are, and that in the end he will make you pay dearly for this!"

"Talk if it so pleases you!" he said.

He grasped her by the arms, and tangled the fingers of the other hand in the pony's mane, and so he led them both along the ravine, following the tiny stream.

Presently they saw a rude hut in the distance, and Sazzac led her toward it, and just before they reached it, the door was opened and a man appeared. He bowed low thrice when he saw them.

"You are Bezo, the goatherd?" Sazzac asked.

"That I am, master."

"I claim the hospitality of thy rude and stinking hut for this lady, who is Dezla, the daughter of the sun."

"Things are not as they should be at the pueblo, my master?"

"They are not, though that is none of your business! I want the maiden kept in safety here, and you shall answer for her with your life. Now, a word with thee, goatherd."

THEY stepped aside a few paces, and Sazzac continued the conversation in whispers.

"The cacique, her father, hath been slain, and the tragedy hath unhinged her mind regarding certain things," he said. "Why, the poor maiden even hath a fancy now and then that I slew the cacique myself. And at one moment she will praise Tanlu, the new general, and the next moment she will call down vengence upon him. You are to pay no attention to what she says, Bezo, and you are to see that she does not escape into the open country."

"If she attempts to leave, how can I detain her, my master? It is not proper that I should put hands on a woman of high birth."

"In such case it is proper, Bezo, for her mind is not her own. And you will be contributing to her safety to do it."

"I understand, master."

"I will be gone a part of the time, for I must go over the hills and observe how things are progressing. But I may return at any instant. Take you the maiden into the hut, and feed her and guard her well, and treat her with kindness, except that she must remain in the hut. You shall be well rewarded."

Then Sazzac glanced back at Dezia once more and hurried up the slope and over the brow of the hill.

Bezo, the goatherd, approached Dezla, not knowing exactly how to act. He had talked to the cacique on several occasions, but here was a noble woman, and it was not the same.

"Will the daughter of the sun honor me by entering my poor hut?" Bezo asked.

He stood back and allowed her to enter first. It was dark inside, but the goatherd threw fuel on the fire and so made the hut bright. In a corner his wife crouched, frightened by the presence of such a noble lady, and a child clung to her.

Dezla sat down in a corner, and called the child to her, and petted it while the woman cooked the food. And all the time her mind was busy.

She ate ravenously when the food and goat's milk were placed before her, and when she had finished she walked to the door of the hut and looked up the ravine, and noticed that Bezo remained a few feet behind her.

"You will please not try to leave the hut, daughter of the sun," he said. "The noble said you were to remain here, and so be safe. My life depends upon it."

"I would not bring you into danger, Bezo," she replied.

"What did Sazzac say to thee?"

"That there was treachery at the pueblo and that your father had been slain."

"That is true, honest goatherd, and none knows it better than Sazzac, for he did the deed."

"Pardon, noble lady, but he mentioned that you would say that. He said that the tragedy had unhinged your mind, and that you fancied peculiar things."

"He is a monster!" she cried. "And he accuses Tanlu of having done the crime! If Tanlu were but here—?"

"You trust Tanlu, noble lady?"

"I do, goatherd. Tanlu discovered that this Sazzac and his nobles plotted to depose my father, and he made it known, and sent the nobles away with the outcast bands. And Sazzac escaped and returned to the pueblo at night, slew my father and carried me away from the temple. Now he says that he will be cacique, and that he will force me to be his wife."

"This is almost past belief," Bezo said.

"Yet it is true, honest goatherd!. My mind is not unhinged! I am the victim of treachery. Is there no one to aid Dezla, the daughter of the sun?"

"If I could be sure—" Bezo began.

"Thou canst not aid me. It would mean death if it was attempted and you failed and fell into Sazzac's hands again. If Tanlu only were here, all would be well!"

"Perhaps I could find this Tanlu, but I cannot go on a journey and watch thee, too."

"Go and find Tanlu, goatherd. I pass you my word that I shall remain here until you return, unless Sazzac comes back and takes me away. The word of a noble woman never is broken, Bezo!"

"I may not find this Tanlu until another sun."

"Do it as quickly as you can. Bezo."

"Sazzac may return and carry thee away."

"That must be chanced."

"He may slay my woman and child, and scatter my flocks."

"I will try to protect your woman and child, and I shall urge him not to stain his hands with the blood of goats."

"Perhaps this Tanlu will not come to thee, being busy doing the work of a great general."

"Whisper into his ear one thing, honest goatherd. Whisper into his ear that Dezla, the daughter of the sun, says that she loves him, and calls upon him to save her."

The face of Bezo brightened.

"That is true, noblewoman?" he gasped.

"It is true!"

"Then am I yours to command, and I know that Tanlu will come to the rescue if I can but find him. I go! But do you try to protect my woman and my flocks."

The daughter of the sun stood in the doorway and watched him go over the crest of the nearest hill and disappear.

"If he meets his death, then I shall starve with our child," the woman behind her moaned.

"Not so!" Dezla of the sun replied. "If he meets

his death, I shall have you taken to the pueblo, and you may spend the remainder of your life there instead of out here in the hills. And if he succeeds, I shall have him returned to the pueblo also, and made a great man, and no longer will he have to herd evil-smelling goats!"

The woman cried out her thanks, for she knew that the daughter of the sun would keep her spoken word.

Meanwhile Sazzac had hurried over the hills until he had reached a certain trail, and down that he hastened toward the pueblo. He left the trail after a time, and crossed another range of hills, and so came where he could see the battle in the distance.

He had left his pony at the hut of Bezo, the goatherd, for a man can hide where a pony cannot; and it was his intention to remain in hiding until he was sure how the battle was going. He had hope that those in the pueblo would be victorious, and that the outcasts would return to aid them in time.

Did this come to pass, then he could appear before his people and claim the right to be cacique. After the fighting was over and they had no further need of Tanlu, they would listen to a noble of their own blood.

If Radzec got the better of the fighting, however, then would Sazzac have another plan to use, for the man thought little of loyalty and only of advancing his own interest.

# CHAPTER XIV

HE watched the distant battle all day, hiding beneath a ledge of rock where the nearest sentinels could not see him. He remained there during the night, too, and just before dawn heard the outcast bands pass on their way back from the Red Pueblo.

When the morning came he saw these outcasts attack Radzec's men from behind, and saw those of the pueblo sally forth to aid them; and while he watched Radzec conducted his retreat to the little hill, and there stood off his foes.

Sazzac could not determine now who was to be the victor in the fighting, and the fact bothered him, for he wished to make no mistake. He wondered whether Tanlu was with the outcasts, whether he had been hurt or slain. And he decided that it was better to find out the truth of the matter.

He removed all the badges of rank that he wore, and put them in a secure hiding place. He threw off his rich blanket of many colors, covered his face and hands with dust and his clothes with dirt, and crept forward.

It took him some time to reach the outskirts of the outcast camp, and when he did it was necessary to hide for a time until he could slip past the sentinels. But finally he found himself near one of the fires and mingled with the men there. The warriors of the several bands were scattered, and they mingled freely with those from the pueblo, and so it was easy for a stranger to avoid suspicion if he guarded his tongue and watched his actions.

Within a short time he heard men speaking of Tanlu.

"Where he is and what he is doing are mysteries," this man said. "He was with us at the Red Pueblo, and the watcher came from this pueblo here and had speech with him. Then he ordered the chieftain who had let a certain noble escape to fall on his own spear, and the chieftain died like a man. Then Tanlu bade us march. I was with the last band, and he told our chieftain that he would not march with us."

"It is a peculiar thing," another said.

"Tanlu has gone about some business of his own, it is supposed. And we need him here. This Radzec is a tougher chieftain than was believed. He has retreated to a position of advantage, and holds it, and we not only are in the open, but also we are exhausted. Unless Tanlu comes, we may have to scatter into the hills."

"And then what will become of those in the pueblo?"

"That is their concern. We already have lost men in their defence. I presume Radzec's warriors will slay them all, and carry away the women. If we are forced to run away, I am for hurrying to the Red Pueblo and taking what loot we can before Radzec returns there."

Now it happened that Sazzac had stumbled upon a band of pessimists, such as may be found here and there in any army, and he made the mistake of taking their views for those of the entire host.

He intended to go about the camp and listen to more, but he saw some men of the pueblo approaching and was afraid that he would be recognized. And did that come to pass he would die, for these men of the chieftain who had fallen upon his own spear at Tanlu's command would make short work of him.

So he slipped away from the fires and in time managed to get by the sentinels, and so hurried back to where he had left his rich blanket and his badges of rank. He bathed himself in a little stream, and, clothed himself again and so looked the noble chieftain once more. And while he did this he thought.

If the people of the pueblo were defeated, Sazzac

would have nobody over whom to be cacique, for Radzec would place there a man of his own choosing. But if Sazzac could earn the regard of Radzec, possibly Radzec would make him a great man. He felt that it was a matter of self-preservation.

How to win the regard of Radzec was a big question, and Sazzac was a considerable time answering it to his own satisfaction. But he found what he supposed was an answer finally, and it cheered him.

He went back toward the little hill again and presently a dark form stood before him, and he knew it for one of Radzec's sentinels.

"It is a friend!" Sazzac called.

"Thy name?"

"Listen well, fellow, for a great deal may depend upon your ears and tongue. I am Sazzac, a great noble of the pueblo! Send word to Radzec, thy cacique, that I wish speech with him, and that I can tell him many things he will be eager to hear."

The sentinel called another, and while this other kept watch over Sazzac the sentinel hurried away with a message. Soon he returned and with him were six warriors, a noble in command of them.

"You are to come to the cacique!" the noble said.

Sazzac went forward, and the warriors surrounded him and led him on up the hill, and so he reached the crest of it and came to the hut that the men had erected for Radzec's use. The noble took him inside.

Radzec crouched on the ground, eating meat, and his eyes blazed as he looked up at Sazzac.

'What does the noble wish?" he asked.

The cacique stood up and grasped his spear, and then motioned for the noble to withdraw.

"Make no treacherous move," he warned, "or I shall slay thee!"

"I will make no treacherous move, O cacique. I have a message for thine ears. alone."

"Say on!"

"I am a noble of high rank, and was second to none except the cacique," Sazzac said. "I loved Dezla, the daughter of the sun, but when it was arranged that she wed your son I smiled and stepped aside, happy in the thought that she was to wed a man more worthy."

He paused a moment to let that sink in, and then continued:

"But your son was foully slain, and it came to the minds of the nobles that the thing had been without our knowledge, and that the cacique had a hand in it. Tanlu, an outcast of the desert and the man who slew thy son, entered the pueblo and was given sanctuary—and then you decided to make war."

"Say on!"

"Then our cacique said that Tanlu was to be the general. We of noble blood could not endure that, and we resented the insult. Tanlu thereupon had us given into the keeping of his outcast bands, for he had called upon them to make war upon you also. They took us when they marched away, and I managed to escape from the chieftain who held me prisoner. These outcasts rode and marched around you as you advanced to attack the pueblo. They went to the Red Pueblo and captured it. They seized your wealth and slew the few guards you had there and the temple maidens killed themselves because of it."

"What is this?" Radzec cried in fury.

"The truth, o cacique! They out-witted you thus!"

"I should have you slain for bringing me such news!"

"You are a man of honor, cacique, and I am of noble blood. And I am here as your guest until this conference is at an end."

"Say on—and your pardon, Sazzac!" Radzec's fury had subsided.

"Having taken your pueblo, these outcasts came back and attacked your force in the rear, according to the plans made by this Tanlu. You know the rest."

"And why are you here, Sazzac?"

"Because I am of noble blood, O cacique! Was it not an insult that this Tanlu was put over me?

"I escaped my captors, as I have said, and crept back into the pueblo at night to take my vengeance. I slew the treacherous cacique—"

"You slew him? That was a good deed, since he ordered the death of my son at an outcast's hands!"

"I did more, great cacique! I carried away with

me, when I left the pueblo, Dezla, the daughter of the sun, the maid who indirectly caused the death of thy prince. Had this maiden looked with favor upon the Prince Lazzano he never would have been slain. And I think that she has forgotten her noble blood, too, and loves this outcast, this Tanlu!"

"Thou art a man who knows how to avenge a wrong!" Radzec cried. "Tell me, do the people of the pueblo love this Dezla?"

"Ha! Do they? They are enraptured of her, oh, cacique! They would die for her!"

"I have a thought," Radzec said, "but am not yet ready to give it utterance. What is your wish of me?"

"I am of noble blood and have been a great chieftain. I would become one of the Red Pueblo. I would have you let me enjoy the rank that is justly mine. I was the most wealthy man in the pueblo, and I would have you return a part of my goods. When you have beaten these outcast dogs, and the pueblo of the east is yours. I would have you send me there to rule in thy name."

"That cannot be done. One of mine own blood must rule."

"Then let me be the second in rank, O cacique!"

"That could be done, Sazzac. But suppose I grant you these things? What will you do to earn them?"

"I will bring into your camp Dezla, the daughter of the sun, the maiden who caused your prince to be slain by an outcast."

"That is well!" Radzec said. "And how can you do such a thing?"

"I have her safe in the hills, guarded by an honest fellow who obeys my word."

Radzec paced back and forth across the floor of the hut. Presently he faced Sazzac again.

"I am a man of my word," he said, "and you are of noble blood. An agreement between us would be observed."

"True, great cacique."

"Bring this daughter of the sun safely to me here, and I will take you into my tribe as a noble, restore your wealth, and allow you to be second in rank in your pueblo. I have spoken. Go!"

Sazzac, a gleam of satisfaction in his eyes, bowed thrice and backed through the doorway. The cacique ordered guards to conduct him to a place where he could escape through the lines. And so Sazzac went his way, not knowing that Radzec had been worrying lest the outcasts and men of the pueblo slay him and all his warriors with the coming of the new day.

As for Radzec, he rubbed his chin with the palm of a hand and paced the floor of his hut, and thought deeply. He fancied that he saw a way out of his present difficulties.

# CHAPTER XV

IT was almost dawn again when Sazzac returned to Bezo's hut, arousing the woman and her child by pounding against the side of the hut with his spear. Dezla already was awake, not having been able to sleep much in such malodorous surroundings.

"We are to go from here, daughter of the sun!" Sazzac said, holding a torch close to her head and looking into her face.

"Let me remain yet awhile; I feel not well," Dezla said; for she thought that perhaps if she could delay Sazzac for a time Tanlu would arrive; and she did not like the look in the noble's face as he bent over her.

"We go at once!" Sazzac said.

He picked her up, carried her out to where the pony was waiting, and lost no time in throwing her across the pony's neck and riding furiously up the ravine.

The dawn came and Sazzac did not even stop the pony to get off with her and worship, at which she wondered much, not knowing that Sazzac feared to look the brilliant god in the face this dawn because of what he was doing.

So they rode through the morning, along ravines and over the crests of hills, and presently they reached the top of a hill from which they could see the battle before them. There Sazzac stopped and dismounted, and put Dezla on the ground also, for he wanted to rest a short time before finishing the journey.

Dezla looked down the slope at the battle and tried to ascertain how things were there.

"Whose camp is at the top of the hill?" she asked.

"That of Radzec," Sazzac said.

"Then our warriors have surrounded him and will be victorious in this fight?"

"Radzec is there because he so wishes to be," Sazzac replied. "He will be victorious."

"Then Tanlu is not here?" she asked.

"He is not here, daughter of the sun!" Sazzac replied; and her hope fled again.

"And what do we here?" she asked. "Is it not dangerous to be so close if Radzec is to win?"

"I have arranged this affair."

"What are you going to do?" she asked in sudden

alarm.

"I am going to repay the dead cacique for having put an outcast over me in rank!" he said. "I am going to repay this Tanlu for having me taken away by one of his bands! I am going to take you to the camp of Radzec."

"He will slay you!"

"I have no fear of that!"

"Then you are traitor and renegade?" she asked. "You have had dealings with this Radzec? You forget the blood that flows in your veins?"

"I have decided!"

"And you would take me as prisoner to Radzec? He will give you honors, I suppose?"

"Assuredly he will, daughter of the sun."

"And what shall become of me?" she asked.

"I know not. That will be Radzec's doing."

"You are giving a daughter of the sun up to insult!" she cried. "Do you not fear to do it? Have you no fear for the just and august brilliant god?"

"I have decided!" he said again.

He turned and looked down the slope toward the scene of battle, and at the crest of the little hill where he could plainly see Radzec's hut. The fight was raging furiously now.

Radzec's warriors were having their fill of fighting that day and great numbers of men were being lost. Slowly the outcasts and the men of the pueblo worked their way up the slope, driving Radzec's men back, while their chieftains and headmen urged them to stand fast. And then they would retire for a short time to get breath and more weapons, and always they brought down more of Radzec's men than they lost of their own.

The great cacique of the Red Pueblo knew that he was fighting for life now, and his warriors knew it, and their desperation increased. The outcasts and pueblo men were battling side by side in harmony to make an end of it. They saw victory just within their grasp and reached out to close their fingers upon it.

But Radzec was bold, and not yet undone. He called his chieftains to him during a lull in the fighting and issued his orders. And the men at the base or the slope suddenly were surprised to see the entire body of Radzec's warriors making a sally, charging down upon them, their warcries ringing among the hills.

The two forces met at the base of the hill with a shock and mingled, and the battle became a maze of individual combats. Radzec's men took a terrible toll this time, but the outcasts remembered the wrongs they had suffered, and started to beat them back. The dead were in heaps among the rocks, and wounded men were screaming, and still the men of the Red Pueblo could not be driven back to the crest of the hill.

Sazzac saw this fighting from another hill and believed that Radzec and his warriors were about to triumph. It was time for him to make his play for favor, he decided.

Before Dezla could speak, he tossed her astride the pony and sprang up behind her and drove the animal down the slope in a rush.

The maze of fighting men did not see him until he was among them, and then they thought that he was connected with one of the forces and was carrying off a prisoner.

Radzec's men were just beginning to fall back as he arrived, for they were unable to face their foes longer. He rode toward them through the ranks of the outcasts, striking with his spear to clear the way.

Up the slope toward the crest of the hill he urged the pony, and the arrows flew about him in a cloud, but he was not hit, and neither was the daughter of the sun nor the beast they rode. He came to the hut and flung himself from his mount, and lifted Dezla to the ground in the midst of a throng of chieftains and headmen where Radzec was seated.

"I have kept faith, O cacique!" Sazzac cried. "Here is Dezla, the daughter of the sun!"

"It is well!" Radzec said. 'Take her into the hut!"

He turned away then to issue orders concerning the defence of the slope, and whispered to his chieftains that there was yet something with which to confound their enemies, and that all hope was not gone. And then he went into the hut himself.

Dezla stood against the wall of it, her hands clasped behind her back, her head erect and a look of haughty pride in her face.

"A beautiful woman!" Radzec exclaimed. "Small wonder that my son was enamored of her! A rare thing for an enemy to have in his hands! You have done well, Sazzac! 1 greet you as chieftain. Take your place outside with my warriors!"

He walked to the door and made known Sazzac's rank, and also that the daughter of the sun was a prisoner, and then he called for two nobles to watch the maiden.

Then Radzec walked a short way down the slope and gave the sign for a parley, and after a little hesitation an outcast chieftain walked forward to have speech with him.

"What is it that the cacique of the Red Pueblo wishes?" he asked. "Are you ready to pray for mercy?"

"Radzec never prays for mercy!" came the answer. "When he is defeated, he dies."

"Then it is time for you to fall upon your own spear, O Radzec!" the outcast cried.

"Not so, scum of the earth! I have certain intelligence for you and your men."

"Say on!"

"Dezla, the beloved daughter of the sun, is a prisoner in my hut at the crest of the hill," Radzec announced. "You saw her come into the camp but a short time ago, fetched by a man on a pony."

"What has that to do with us? Are you boasting of the fact that you make war on women?"

"I have come to tell you that you will withdraw your forces," Radzec said. "The men of the pueblo will return there immediately, and the outcasts will go there also and camp at the foot of the pueblo. Then will I march my warriors down the hill and to the Red Pueblo, and this fighting will be at an end. If aught at the Red Pueblo has been harmed by the men of the open country during my absence, as I have heard, I will send warriors into the hills to punish the outcasts they may find. That much is understood!"

"We have heard. But why should we do these things when you are on the verge of defeat?"

"Because I have Dezla, the daughter of the sun, in my hands. And if these things are not done as I order, then will I work my vengeance upon her. I have a sun priest here with me, and I shall give this fair maiden of noble birth to the lowest goatherd among my men, and have her wedded to him.

"And after they have been wedded a short time, so that she will appreciate the indignity, I will take her away from the goatherd and make her a common slave of the pueblo, to be kicked and cuffed, and you may be sure that men and women will kick and cuff her gladly, knowing what she has been."

He ceased speaking, and the man below him

laughed, and the outcasts who had heard laughed also. But there was a sudden tumult among the men of the eastern pueblo, and they crowded forward crying out against being compelled to endure such a thing.

"Derla is our daughter of the sun!" they cried. "We cannot let her be made to suffer such indignities. Do the bidding of Radzec!"

"Wait!" the outcast commanded, and then he shouted to Radzec again. "How can you do these things?" he asked. "If we continue fighting, you shall be defeated and will have no chance to wed Dezla to a goatherd."

"If you do not agree and allow us to return to the Red Pueblo, I will slay this Dezla with my own knife!" Radzec replied.

"And if we agree, what then?"

"I shall take this Dezla with us, to make sure you do not attack us on the way. If you do, she dies. If you keep the agreement, I will have her returned to the pueblo as soon as my men are safe at home."

"And could we believe you?" the outcast chieftain sneered. "Could any word of the detestable Radzec be believed? More like you would use this means to get safe at the Red Pueblo and then work your vengeance on Dezla."

"I have stated the case," Radzec said. "What is your answer?"

Again the men of the eastern pueblo crowded

around the outcast chieftains, begging earnestly that they make such an agreement.

"The brilliant god will smite us if we allow Dezla to be offered indignity!" they cried. "That Radzec and his warriors escape is better than that Dezla be harmed."

"We cannot make the agreement," one of the outcasts said. "Here we have a chance to end Radzec's cruelty and injustice forever, and it is a chance not to be rejected. It is better that one woman be shown indignity or die than that a tyrant rule."

"Make the agreement!" they begged. "We cannot fight while Dezla is held prisoner!"

"How is this?"

"To fight at such a time," said one of the pueblo men, "would be to take part blame for what may happen to the maiden. We shall hold ourselves blameless in the sight of the brilliant god!"

"You would turn against us, your allies?"

"Not so! We will retire down the hill and refuse to fight at all."

"So be it!" the outcast leader cried. "We fight alone, and when we have defeated Radzec all glory and loot shall be ours!"

Then he turned up the hill again and made Radzec his answer.

"We come to no such agreement, O cacique! We will fight on!"

"Then I wed Dezla to a goatherd when you have

been vanquished, and I will torture those of you my men capture while the priest is saying the ceremony. And should you defeat us, Dezla of the sun dies by my own hand!"

The chieftain raised his hand, and his men charged forward, and the battle was on again. But the outcasts found themselves more than evenly numbered now, with the men of the pueblo sulking in the rear and refusing to bear their part of the combat, and Radzec's men drove them back down the hill.

There at the base of the hill they made their stand, and there, during the afternoon, many of them died, and others were sorely wounded, but still they fought savagely, knowing what they might expect if Radzec's warriors defeated them.

They urged the men of the pueblo to join in the combat, but they would not. They wondered why Tanlu did not appear to lead them to victory. They began to lose hope, but still they fought and bled and died, and meanwhile took their toll of Radzec's men.

They charged, and for a time gained an advantage, and the chieftains under Radzec called upon their warriors to make a stand.

Their numbers were about even, and Radzec held the advantage of position. His archers poured down clouds of arrows upon those in the rear, driving them forward, and when they were driven forward the warriors with the spears met them.

"Something must happen, or we are lost!" cried one of the headmen of the outcasts.

And something did!

## CHAPTER XVI

DEZLA heard the din of battle, as she had heard the conversation of the cacique and the headman of the outcasts.

She realized that the men of the pueblo had ceased fighting because of what it might mean to her, and knew that the outcasts, therefore, were hard pressed.

After a time the two nobles who had been assigned to guard her went to the doorway to watch the fighting. She crept after them and crouched near the wall not far away, her head in her hands, as if frightened. The nobles regarded her and believed she had no thought save that of fear for her own future.

They stepped outside, shouting to the men fighting below and urging them to greater efforts, and soon were a short distance from the door, all thought of Dezla of the sun forgotten.

Dezla crept to the skins over the doorway and held them back, and glanced out.

The slope was filled with maddened, fighting men. Not far from the hut Sazzac was conferring with another chieftain regarding the battle. Not a man but had his back turned toward her.

She saw Sazzac's pony a short distance from the door and ran forward to the pony. In an instant she was upon the beast's back. She stuck her heels into his flanks and shouted into his ear.

Down the slope the frightened pony raced, knocking warriors out of his path, rushing straight toward the fighting outcasts. Men struck at her as she flew past, but none gave her a wound.

And then the pony charged through the front of the fighting, and she found herself surrounded entirely by the outcasts.

"Ho, men of the eastern pueblo!" she shrieked. "To arms! Fight for your honor! Dezla of the sun has escaped Radzec! Dezla of the sun leads you!"

The sulking warriors of the pueblo sprang to their feet and regarded her with astonishment. And then some recognized her and shouted her name, and they grasped bows and spears and charged forward, alive with inspiration now that the daughter of the sun was their leader.

They shouted their war-cries and ran to the aid of the outcasts, and hurled themselves upon

Radzec's tired men like thunderbolts. It was useless for the cacique of the Red Pueblo to call upon his forces to stand, for they could not, before such an onslaught. They gave ground, and then broke and ran.

The men of the eastern pueblo pursued, and the outcasts with them, and they carried Dezla of the sun along with them. She continued to shriek at them her encouragement, urging them to an immediate victory. Up on the hill Radzec's archers sent a flock of arrows that struck down many, and the charge was halted for the moment.

In that moment, the men of the pueblo surged around their daughter of the sun, cheering her madly. The frightened pony reared and plunged, and men tried to grasp its mane. And then it backed away, giving little squeals of fear, and bolted.

Its nose was pointed toward the crest of the hill, and that way it ran. Dezla of the sun was dazed for a moment, and then realized what was taking place. She would have thrown herself from the pony's back, but it was too late. Already the beast had carried her among the warriors of Radzec.

## CHAPTER XVII

THEY seized her and carried her before the cacique, and he ordered her put into the hut again and designated two more nobles to guard her, having slain the two who had allowed her to escape. This was the moment, Radzec knew, to charge again. For now that the daughter of the sun was once more in the cacique's power, the men of the eastern pueblo refused to continue fighting.

They hurried to the rear, carrying the curses of the outcasts with them, and Radzec's warriors charged again.

But the outcasts were not to be beaten back and scattered that easily. They stood in their tracks, and either died or made some of the cacique's warriors die. Radzec hurled upon them some men he had been holding in reserve, and they gave ground. Back down the slope they were forced, prevented from fleeing only by the taunts of their headmen.

It seemed the end, and that Radzec would win. The brilliant god was dropping behind the hills to the westward, and soon it would be too dark to fight longer. If they could not hold their lines until the darkness came, they would be beaten.

Then they heard a sudden tumult behind them, and feared for a moment that the men of the eastern pueblo were turning upon them, or that some of Radzec's allies had arrived.

But those nearest the rear saw three men riding like the wind into the battle, bending low over their ponies, and they heard the cry of the pueblo men: "Tanlu! Tanlu has come!"

Like a whirlwind he was among them, and the watcher and Bezo, who had ridden with him, were left behind. The outcasts cheered him, and followed him to the front. He sprang from his pony, and singled out one of Radzec's chieftains, and slew him. He called for men to follow, and charged up the hill. And the outcasts rallied and went after him, forcing the cacique's warriors back foot by foot, until finally they broke and fled.

Radzec, calling down curses upon the head of Tanlu, knew that nothing more could be accomplished that day. He allowed the outcasts to retire and arrange their lines. He put out his own guards, and told the men to light fires and cook meat. And then he went into his hut, where Dezla of the sun crouched against the wall, feeling a little hope and a great deal of happiness because the shouts had told her that Tanlu had come.

Tanlu, the outcast, issued his orders quickly, and then hurried to the rear where the men of the pueblo were gathered.

"How is it you were not in the fighting?" he demanded, and there was rage in his voice.

"Why should you ask?" one demanded. "Why should we allow you to stand before us alive? You obtained sanctuary by a trick and brought on this conflict. You had our nobles scattered among your outcast tribes. Then you slipped away and left us without a leader, and before you went you took the life of our old cacique, and carried away Dezla of the sun."

"Fools of little faith! I departed from the pueblo because it was my right, and for a very good fighting man's reason. I hurried to the Red Pueblo to send back these your allies to aid you. Your cacique was slain by Sazzac, a noble of your own blood."

"That does not ring true!"

"Yes, it is the truth!" said a man who stood at Tanlu's side.

They looked at this man and saw that he was Bruxoli, the watcher, for whom they had great respect.

"1, too, believe the tale!" the watcher said. "I left the pueblo to follow the trail of this Tanlu, and when l found him I meant to slay him if he had done these things. And I found that he had not, and that Sazzac had.

"Sazzac carried the daughter of the sun to the hut of this goatherd here, which marks him the guilty man. This Bezo started out to find Tanlu at the maiden's bidding, and he met us while Tanlu and I were seeking Sazzac and the maiden. We returned to Bezo's hut, and there found that Sazzac had returned and taken the maiden away."

"Then must we bow our necks to Tanlu for having misjudged him," said one of the pueblo men.

"And why have you not been fighting?" Tanlu cried. "Why have you left your allies to bear the brunt of the conflict? Is that the part of honorable and brave men?"

"Do you not know? Because Dezla of the sun is in the hands of Radzec, and he has said he would offer her indignities if we do not retire and allow him to escape to his own pueblo. So we could take no part in the fighting."

"How is this?" Tanlu cried in a terrible voice.

"It is true O Tanlu!" one of the outcast headmen told him. "But we fought on. The maiden escaped and came to lead us, and then her pony bolted and took her back to the crest of the hill again."

"She is in Radzec's hands?" Tanlu cried.

"In the hands of the cacique of the Red Pueblo?" the watcher demanded.

"Even so, honored ones!"

Tanlu turned away from them to hide his emotion, and the watcher followed him aside.

For a time he paced back and forth before the fire, while the men of the pueblo and the outcasts waited, the former eager to do his bidding now that they knew they had misjudged him, the latter glad that their leader had arrived and sure he would lead them to a victory.

Presently Tanlu called the chieftains and headmen to him.

"How goes the battle?" he asked.

"Badly, Tanlu," one of them reported. "We had Radzec in sore straits before the maiden was delivered into his hands, but since then the men of the pueblo will not fight."

"How came Dezla of the sun in the hands of the cacique?"

"Sazzac has turned renegade. As we fought he rode through us on a pony, and the maiden was before him on the beast, and he carried her thus to the crest of the hill."

Tanlu turned to the man who represented those of the pueblo.

"If we all fight, we can slay this Radzec and his entire band," he said. "The constant menace of him will not then be over the land. Already have the outcasts captured the Red Pueblo and taken much loot. If Radzec is defeated here, and his men slain or made slaves or scattered, I will have these outcast friends of mine share the loot with you of the eastern pueblo."

"We cannot fight when Dezla of the sun is in their hands," the man replied. "That would be the same as aiding in offering her indignity."

"But if the daughter of the sun was free? If she were taken from Radzec's hut and brought here among you?" Tanlu asked.

"Then would we fight like wild men, oh. Tanlu. Then we would slay Radzec and his men and wipe them from the face of the land!"

"It is a long time until the dawn, and many things can happen." Tanlu said. "Do you aid the outcasts in keeping guard tonight. When the dawn comes we shall see what the night has brought!"

Tanlu walked away then, and Bruxoli, the watcher, followed him, because he guessed that Tanlu wished it, and Bezo, the goatherd, remained some distance behind, but followed also, not knowing what else to do.

Tanlu led the way to a jumble of rocks in the darkness beside a dry watercourse, and there he sat down and motioned for Bruxoli to sit down also.

"This is a sorry business!" the watcher said. "If the brilliant god is good to me and allows me to meet this Sazzac—"

"Sazzac comes to my spear!" Tanlu interrupted. "Did not the daughter of the sun tell the goutherd that in her heart there was love for Tanlu? So it is my right!"

"Then may I be at your side to aid if you need it?"

"I shall not need aid, though I thank thee for offering it! When Sazzac stands before me he is as good as a dead man!"

"Dezla of the sun is in the hut of the cacique of the Red Pueblo, O Tanlu! What are we to do?"

"Rescue her!" Tanlu said.

"Enter his camp at night, and go into his hut, with his chieftains sleeping around him and the guards alert?"

"Yes! Do you think it cannot be done?"

"I have not said so. At least it may be attempted. I may go with you?"

"That is granted. And the goatherd also."

"What are your plans, Tanlu?"

"I will select half a dozen men of valor whom I can trust. All of us will tear our clothing and remove all badges of rank. We will smear dirt upon our faces. Let that be done, and the rest will follow."

He sent Bezo with a message that brought half a dozen of the outcasts to his side, and to them he explained the matter; and all agreed that it was an excellent plan so far, and were eager for the adventure and their part in it.

So they removed all badges of rank, and threw dirt upon their bodies and smeared blood and dust upon their faces. Standing in the light of one of the fires they looked at one another, and found that they appeared as humble warriors who had fought hard during the day and were almost exhausted.

Then, without speaking a word, Tanlu led the way out of the camp, the others following him silently, the goatherd last of all, as became him.

## CHAPTER XVIII

THEY made excellent progress, yet without noise, circling the hill and approaching it from the rear.

"We will scatter now and climb each in his own manner, except that the watcher and Bezo will remain close to me," Tanlu said. "We shall slip past their sleepy sentinels and creep into the camp. All shall lie down near a fire. and gradually arouse and go forward until in the vicinity of Radzec's hut."

"That is understood, Tanlu."

"I shall watch my chance to rush into the hut and rescue the daughter of the sun. At the same time, the watcher and Bezo will start a tumult. You others will spring up crying that there is an attack being made in the night, and gather your weapons and rush down the hill as if to aid in warding it off.

"That will cause a commotion, and during it I

shall escape with the maiden, the watcher and Bezo aiding me. You others will charge down the hill and into our own ranks, and so will be safe."

"It is an excellent plan!" one said.

"I shall give you ample time to work near the hut. If any man is recognized as an enemy and captured, he will know how to die with his lips closed."

"That, too, is understood before it is spoken, Tanlu."

"It is well!" Tanlu said.

He left them then, with the watcher and Bezo following him, and they scattered and made their way up the side of the steep hill, being careful to make not the slightest noise.

One by one they slipped past the sentinels and stretched on the ground before the nearest fire, except that the watcher had to slay a guard who feared something was wrong and was about to sound an alarm. And then they began following Tanlu's instructions, mingling with the sleeping men, getting up now and then and going to another fire as if wishing to sleep near comrades they liked, but always working closer to the hut of the cacique.

Tanlu and the watcher and Bezo got finally to the big fire before the hut, and lay down a short distance from the nobles, who were enjoying the sleep of exhausted men.

There they remained for a time, to give the others a chance to draw near, and also to look over the ground.

Half a score of men were at the nearest blaze, the most of them chieftains of high rank. Before the door of the hut a guard was fighting himself to keep awake. From the interior came the sound of voices, and Tanlu judged that Radzec was discussing the situation with one of his trusted lieutenants. He looked in vain for Sazzac.

After a time he bade the watcher and Bezo remain quiet, and then like a snake he wriggled away from the fire until he was in deep darkness; and then he turned toward the hut again and approached it on the dark side, keeping it between himself and the fire.

The hut was but a temporary one constructed for the shelter of the cacique. Tanlu stretched himself beside the rear wall and began digging with his fingers. The work was slow, for the slightest noise might have caused disaster.

In time he had a tiny hole beneath the wall, and he bent his head and peered inside.

Radzec was squatting in the middle of the structure. a chieftain at his side. Two nobles were near the doorway. Dezla of the sun was crouched in a corner, her eyes wide open, and anger blazing in them.

"It is the only way," Radzec was saying. "If the men of pueblo fight with the outcasts when dawn comes, we shall be defeated. Our men are weary, and their ranks are grown thin. They cannot battle much longer to any advantage."

"Can we escape and reach the Red Pueblo, we can defend ourselves there, and gather strength, and having gathered it attack these folk again and make them pay," the chieftain said.

"That is my thought!" the cacique replied. "We have paid too dearly in this campaign."

"Thy plans, then?"

"We shall awaken the men without causing a great disturbance. We shall slip down the rear of the hill to the ravine thou last mentioned as having seen. Swiftly we shall creep along it leaving our fires burning here and the few guards watching the foe to the front. The guards will meet death later, of course, but a few men must be sacrificed."

"Of course," the chieftain agreed.

"When the dawn comes our enemies will find only the ashes of our fires and the few guards. By that time we shall be far on our way. Perhaps they will pursue, but we will be in the lead and can travel swiftly, and they will be somewhat exhausted by following and catching up with us. If they do so, and we must give battle, at least we will be as able to give it there as here. And here there can be no advantage to us at all."

"It is an excellent plan," the chieftain agreed. "And what of the daughter of the sun?"

"She shall be taken with us. I do hold her to

blame for all this sorry business. Had she loved my son and wanted him, he would not have been slain."

"Then I will awaken the chieftains and give them news of your plan, and the men shall begin to creep away down the back of the hill," the noble said. "The fools of outcasts never thought to put sentinels in our rear, thinking we would not try to leave that way."

The chieftain got up.

"And what of this Sazzac?" he asked as he reached the doorway.

"He was traitor and renegade to his own people, hence cannot be trusted by us," Radzec said. "After we have used him, he shall have his throat slit some night as he sleeps."

Now Tanlu crept away from the hut and circled through the darkness and so reached the watcher and Bezo again, for he knew that there was little time. What he wished to do could not be accomplished so easily if the men were awake, for then they would be alert, whereas, he knew, men coming from a sound sleep to find a tumult run this way and that and do little or nothing until it is too late.

"The time has come!" he told them. "Do you make the commotion when I clap my hands."

He hurried back to the rear of the hut and saw that the chieftain was on the point of leaving to awaken the others, and so he clapped his hands softly.

The watcher and Bezo sprang to their feet and began shrieking, and the other men at the fires near by did likewise, and suddenly the air of the night was filled with clamor. Warriors sprang to their feet, trying to scratch the sleep out of their eyes, and grasping for their weapons, tumbling over one another, fighting one another, and in an instant the camp was a scene of confusion.

"The outcasts are upon us! The outcasts are upon us!" Tanlu's friends cried.

And they grasped spears and began to charge down the hill, and the warriors of Radzec, not awaiting word from their chieftains, followed in the wake of Tanlu's men.

Tanlu grasped a section of the rear wall of the hut and waited. He saw the two nobles inside spring to the doorway, and saw the cacique thrust them aside and run out, calling upon his chieftains to know the reason for the tumult. He heard the cries that the outcasts were attacking, and began shrieking his orders.

Tanlu tugged at the section of wall, and it gave way, and he sprang into the hut. One of the nobles went down with a knife through his heart, and Tanlu sprang for the other, and slew him also.

"Come, daughter of the sun!" he cried.

He grasped her by the hands, not even hearing her glad cry of welcome, and so urged her through the hole in the wall and to the rear of the hut. There he picked her up in his strong arms, and rushed away through the darkness. and the watcher ran on one side of him and Bezo, the goatherd, on the other.

Radzec's men were almost at the bottom of the slope now. Down below the guards and sentinels had given the alarm, and the outcasts, thinking that the cacique was attempting a night attack, rushed forward to give battle.

"Tanlu! Fight for Tanlu!" they cried.

And Tanlu was running down the hill, still carrying Dezla of the sun in his arms, and his two friends running beside him. Here the ground was rough and unknown, and there was much stumbling, but they made excellent progress.

Fresh fuel had been thrown on the fires, and now it was almost as light as day, and as he ran Tanlu saw that the outcasts had clashed with Radzec's men and were fighting furiously, and that the men of the pueblo still hung about the rear and refused to take part in the combat, thinking that Dezla of the sun still was a prisoner in Radzec's camp.

It came to Tanlu's mind then that here was the chance to make an end of it, if only he could get the men of the pueblo to fight. And the only way to do that, he knew, was to place the daughter of the sun in their midst and urge them to settle the score.

Now he was obliged to run closer to the fighting, frantic men, for he had come to the edge of a ravine into which he could not drop in the darkness without fear of wrenching a leg or breaking an arm, and injuring Dezla also.

He put the maiden down on the ground, and called upon the watcher and the goatherd to watch either side of her and shield her from harm, and so they rushed on, Tanlu leading the way.

They reached the edge of the combat, and Tanlu's spear soon was red on its point, and then it snapped off close and he threw it away and clasped his knife of flint. And so he came face to face with Sazzac!

Sazzac was fighting for his life with two of the outcast headmen opposed to him. He knew there was nothing in life for him did Radzec suffer defeat, and there was nothing if Radzec won, though he did not know that. And so he fought with all his skill against the very men with whom he should have been allied, the picture of a traitor and renegade.

Tanlu shrieked at the two men Sazzac opposed, and they fell back, and the treacherous noble found himself confronted by an infuriated man with a demon glaring from his eyes.

He felt that his time had come, and started to raise his spear.

But Tanlu grasped him about the arms and swung his body over his head, and crashed him down to the rocks and stunned him and then he picked him up again and carried him across his broad shoulders as he ran.

So they got Dezla of the sun through the fore-front of the fighting and to a place of comparative security. Tanlu pushed the watcher aside and looked at the men of the pueblo, and they looked at him, and at the daughter of the sun.

"Laggards!" Tanlu shrieked. "Here is Dezla, thy goddess, rescued by me from the hut of Radzec. Will you fight now? Will you aid the outcasts? Will you seize this advantage and be rid of the menace of Radzec forever?"

Their shouts answered him, and they charged past him in a frenzy and hurled themselves upon Radzec's men, and the outcasts welcomed their coming with a chorus of cheers. Tanlu called half a dozen to guard Dezla, and bade the watcher call half a dozen, more to keep Sazzac from escaping until he returned, and then rushed away.

NOW was he general in truth, for he charged to the front and seized a spear from a wounded man, and began execution. His orders rang out above the din of battle. He called upon the outcasts and the men of the pueblo for an extra effort. Before that terrific onslaught Radzec's warriors fell back, fighting every foot of the way—fell back up the slope toward their fires on the crest of the hill.

For there was no stopping Tanlu's men now. The outcasts fought out of pure joy in his leadership, and

the men of the eastern pueblo fought like insane be-
ings because of the affront Radzec had shown Dezla
of the sun. And they gave no quarter and took no
prisoners, but drove the cacique's men back and
back, save those who dropped lifeless here and
there.

More fuel was thrown upon the fires, and a band
of the outcasts went around the flank to prevent
their enemies escaping in the rear. Radzec stood on
the crest of the hill with his men hedged in around
him, and there he issued his orders and fought as
well as he might. And the circle of his defenders
grew smaller and smaller as the cheers of the victor
rang out.

Radzec thought of the cruelty of his rule, of the
ignoble things he had done to men; and his foes
thought of them, too. He remembered how he had
slain entire tribes for the pure love of it, and without
any real grievance whatever, and began to fear for
what fate had in store for him.

Radzec saw his chieftains slain before him. He
saw his men dropping as the outcasts rushed in. He
threw up his hands in token of surrender, and
shrieked so that all might hear.

"Mercy! Mercy!" he cried.

An outcast thrust a spear into his side, and that
was all the mercy he obtained, being spared torture
on the morrow. And so Radzec died, and the few of
his warriors remaining lost heart and stood still

while death came to them.

Then there was a pause, and then the air was rent with shrieks of victory. Tanlu was seized by strong hands and tossed into the air, and they hailed him a great general. But Tanlu was thinking of other things, and he hurried down the slope again, and came to the place where Dezla of the sun was resting, and where Sazzac was being held prisoner.

"We meet, Sazzac!" he cried. "Traitor to your cacique, defiler of the temple, we meet! Treacherous noble—"

"Dog, and associate of a goatherd!" Sazzac snarled.

"You hope to taunt me into taking your life suddenly? You hope to die from a single violent blow? I remember, Sazzac, that once you were an honorable man of good blood, and so will give you the chance of combat. It shall be with flint knives, Sazzac!"

One of the men handed Sazzac a knife, and the others stepped back. And Tanlu grasped his own knife and rushed in, and they circled, both fighting for life and knowing it.

But in Sazzac's heart there was only the desire to slay this man, and with it the knowledge that he could not escape if he did, while in Tanlu's was a great rage because of the wrongs the man before him had done, the greatest being that he had offered affront to the daughter of the sun.

And so Sazzac could not hope to stand long before Tanlu. But he fought as well as he could, though it seemed that Tanlu touched him when he willed. Sazzac felt his arms being slashed, felt the knife rip across his breast, felt it tear at his sides. He backed away, advanced, stepped to either side and circled, and always Tanlu darted in and his knife left another mark.

And then a great fear came into the breast of Sazzac, for he realized what Tanlu was doing. Sazzac knew the man was playing with him, that he was slashing him as he would have slashed a goatskin, that he was not trying to have a quick end of it, but was torturing, taking Sazzac's lifeblood drop by drop.

For a short time longer they fought, and still Tanlu cut and slashed when he would, and sneered at times because of the poor skill Sazzac displayed. Then Sazzac became like a madman, not able longer to endure the punishment. and he dropped his knife to the ground, and shrieked in agony and turned to flee.

Tanlu sprang after him—and his flint knife went home!

"Die, Sazzac!" he cried. "Die, treasonable dog! Renegade, defiler of the sun temple, die the death! And so may all such die, whether their blood be noble or poor!"

And then he turned and looked into the eyes of the daughter of the sun.

"Dezla," he said.

"My lord?"

"Radzec's warriors are vanquished, and the eastern pueblo has been saved. I am happy to have been of service to thee."

"And now?" she asked.

"Now I shall go back into the open country, and perhaps at times I shall come to the pueblo and you will be kind enough to smile upon me for these things that I have done."

"You go back to the open country?" she asked. "But I think it would be much better to live in the pueblo."

"Why should I?" he asked.

"Dezla sent word that she had given you her love."

"Was it sent because of your peril, daughter of the sun, or because your heart spoke?"

"My heart spoke, O Tanlu! It speaks to thee now!"

Then Tanlu gave a glad cry and sprang forward and took the daughter of the sun in his arms, and the outcasts and the men of the pueblo gathered around to cheer them.

"If a priest survives, we can be wed at dawn," Dezla said. "For it is but a small distance to the pueblo and there are ponies to ride."

"Let us start!" Tanlu said.

"In our happiness we must not forget others. O Tanlu. Many men have died, and there will be women and children mourning. And even I must mourn, for my father is no more."

"And we have no cacique!" the watcher said. "Nor have we nobles, since all proved traitors, though some of them will be forgiven now because they fought so well."

"Nor has the Red Pueblo a cacique!" Bezo put in boldly, almost afraid to hear his own voice in such company.

"A true word!" the watcher cried. "And none of the nobles of the Red Pueblo live. Both pueblos need a cacique, some strong man who can rule justly and keep enemies away through fear."

"And where can we find such a one?" a chieftain asked.

"There is but one—Tanlu!" Bruxoli cried.

It was a proper thought. They took up the cry— the outcasts and the men of the eastern pueblo, and Tanlu knew it was their wish and so should be cheerfully obeyed.

"It is well!" he said. "I shall wed the daughter of the sun, and I shall be cacique of both pueblos. And these men who have been called outcasts shall be outcasts no longer, but shall go to the Red Pueblo and people it, apportioning the loot. I shall dwell in the eastern pueblo with my wife. Bezo, honest goat-herd, cleanse yourself in the river and then have the priest bless you, and I shall make you a noble, for you have served the daughter of the sun. Bruxoli, good watcher, thou hast been a loyal friend. If you would rule the Red Pueblo under my guidance—"

"Pardon, Tanlu, but I am the watcher!" Bruxoli said. "I love to watch from the summit of the lookout rock, watch the trails, and over those in the pueblo. And Dezla of the sun will be in the pueblo."

"I understand, good friend," Tanlu said, clasping him by the hand in the sign of friendship. "It shall be as you wish, for you are a loyal man. Watch—and help me watch over the daughter of the sun, for we both love her."

And so they started for the pueblo, and arrived safely.

And when the dawn touched the eastern mountains with glory, Bruxoli stood like a bronze statue on the summit of the lookout rock and gave the signal, and far below him the great gong struck on the roof of the temple. And Tanlu clasped the daughter of the sun in his arms and looked upward, but Braxoli gave them never a glance. He was alone, high in the world, with his thoughts and his aching heart, yet glad that the daughter of the sun was to mate with a worthy man.

And so we leave him as we found him, a stalwart bronze statue outlined against the brightening sky.

## THE END

# TO THE READER

If you enjoyed this book, you will be glad to know that there are many others just as well written, just as interesting, to be had in the Fiction House Press Library.

You will find the Fiction House Press Library online at

www.FictionHousePress.com

www.ingramcontent.com/pod-product-compliance
Lightning Source LLC
Chambersburg PA
CBHW030546030726
47495CB00004B/1151